ORANGE SWIRL

HARET CHRONICLES QILIN: SUGAR BITES THREE

LAUREL CHASE

ISBN: 9798677276750

DEDICATION

This series is for all the girls who like sex and sugar.

So, that's everyone, right?

Carry on.

CHAPTER ONE

CARLYLE

"Try it now," I suggested, settling my hands on my hips and cocking my head at Dair through the doorway. He was in for a shock, this time - I'd been working hard on this trick.

My mage only raised an eyebrow and focused on the room I was occupying, summoning his siphoning magic and popping out of view.

"Sorry, Cariño. It didn't work," he said as he reappeared, standing exactly where he'd been before.

"Didn't it, though? Check yourself again." I

grinned, holding out my hand to him.

He reached to grasp it, but of course he missed. Because he was still in the hallway, not in my bedroom like the glamor was telling him. Yep. Qilin mind tricks, next level.

"What the fuck?" he muttered, staring down at his empty fingers. "But you're right here."

I powered down the glamor a bit. He cursed again as the illusion flickered around him, and he realized he'd siphoned exactly nowhere. He glared at the doorway that still separated us, and my grin got even bigger.

"See, that's the beauty of the trick. We can't seem to get the physical barriers to work against mages, so I made a mental block. They'll think they've siphoned in, but really any siphoning magic just triggers the glamor. We can put this around the outside of the castle, and it'll act like a force field. I'm sure Jai can rig up some sort of warning bell for us, or trap or something, so we can go get the intruders before they figure it out."

"It's brilliant, Carlyle," Dair said, a genuine smile replacing the glower on his handsome face. I felt my cheeks flush with the compliment. We'd been looking for a way to keep random mages - like Dair's mother - from bypassing our security and siphoning into the castle. For whatever weird reason, none of the usual methods had proved effective.

"But can't I just walk right in?" he asked, his body swaying forward. His lush lips popped open when he realized he was getting exactly nowhere with that tactic, too.

"Same principle - the glamor tricks your mind *and* your magic into thinking you're inside. I know I'm supposed to be unmixing my magic, but it's just too handy," I confessed, falling backward onto the bed. A fae might be able to break the glamor, but none of the mages would have the right power. I felt a supreme satisfaction that I was protecting my men and the small assembly of shifters who had gathered under our roof for shelter and employment. It felt awesome to keep them all safe with my magic and my smarts.

Lifting my head, I considered the fact that Dair was still stuck outside the room, twisted in my web of glamor.

A sly thought entered my mind, and I wriggled all the way back onto the bed. Kneeling, I locked my mage in my gaze. I started swiveling my hips and peeling up my shirt, inch by inch.

Dair sort of growled as the grin dropped from his face, giving him a distinctly predatory look. His hands clenched the door frame he couldn't get through, and I blew him an air kiss.

I dropped the shirt beside me on the bed and ran my hands down my sides, dragging my thumbs over the cups of my lavender-colored lacy bra - an embarrassingly expensive one he'd brought me from Patriam. It matched my eyes exactly, but I doubted Dair was thinking about my eyes as I pinched my nipples.

"Just what do you think you're doing," he warned, as I slid my palms lower and hooked my fingers into the waistband of my leggings.

"Just giving you some incentive to *really* test that barrier," I teased, shimmying the leggings down past my hips. It wouldn't work, of course. I'd have to drop the glamor - but only after I'd had my fun.

I thought Dair growled again, but suddenly we both snapped our attention to an actual growl beyond the hallway. A growl which was immediately followed by a furious roar.

"Sol!" I gasped, yanking my clothes back on and dropping the glamor in an instant. Dair and I hurried to trace the sound, which had been matched by shouting now.

Shouting that sounded suspiciously like…

"Jai!" I yelled as we skidded into the library, just in time to see my vampire pin a half-shifted Sol against a heavy wooden shelf. "Get a goddamn grip!"

Jai snarled, but he dropped his hold on my lion and backed away. His eyes were fully black, and his fangs had extended well past his upper lip.

"What the actual fuck is going on here?" I demanded, my eyes narrowed on the pair of them.

Sol shook his head in a very animalistic way, drawing his shifted mane and claws back inside. He looked positively murderous.

"The boss didn't take well to my advice," he hissed, and I blinked at him. I knew Sol wasn't always like a kitten in the sun, of course. But I'd never seen him turn that kind of ferocity on any of the team, especially Jai.

"What the hell kind of advice?" I stammered.

"Where Carlyle goes, I go," Jai said, and I got the sense he'd repeated that a few times already.

"The pride lands are no place for a goddamn vampire right now," Sol yelled, throwing his hands up like he'd also made that point before this. He stalked from the room, brushing past me with a growled apology that sounded suspiciously like it doubled as an insult to Jai.

I sighed and turned on my vampire. "Are you being an overprotective dick again?"

Jai slitted his eyes at me, and I knew I'd called it. My vampire had a serious hero complex, and no amount of me demonstrating my magic's strength or creativity would ever change that.

"I don't want you going to the pride lands without my protection," he insisted.

Dair slid me a worried look. "Boss, perhaps a bit of diplomacy might-"

"Fuck diplomacy!" Jai roared, sounding like a teenager ranting against the government.

Obviously, this disagreement called for a different kind of diplomatic persuasion. I walked to him and wrapped my arms around his waist, gazing up into his dark eyes. "Hey, let's just talk about it, yeah? Why is Sol so worried?"

I wanted to go after my lion too, but I figured Jai would just stalk right behind me, making things worse. Instead, I sent Dair a quick thought to check on Sol, and my mage nodded, tossing me a look that said good luck chatting with the boss.

Jai tensed and glared after him, only looking back down at me when the library door clicked shut. I was running my nails gently up and down his spine, and he gradually relaxed a little into my touch.

"The shifters here in the castle have been hearing reports of vampire attacks in areas much too far from Saori Sang - horrific slaughters and blood drainings," he admitted in a guilt-stricken voice, and I sucked in a breath.

"Shit," I whispered, resting my forehead on his chest. "Remember, Jai. Their actions *aren't* yours."

We knew his aunt Merden had been up to some nasty things in Saori Sang since she'd claimed the throne, but we'd been too preoccupied to deal with them. We still were, to be honest.

Fear flooded my belly as I imagined Jai rushing off to battle for his family throne, and I understood it was probably the same instinct that led him to pick a fight with Sol.

The realization really didn't help our current situation, though.

"Don't worry, *aima*. My priority is with you, and you alone. Besides, if Merden is to be replaced according to our customs, it is Kana's birthright to do so - otherwise Saori Sang may descend even deeper into chaos."

I leaned back to consider his expression. I could

tell the words cost him, even though I hadn't pried enough to understand their meaning. "Have you heard anything from her?" I asked instead. Damn, I missed that girl.

Jai sighed. "I've sent messages to Grand-mere each time one of our staff goes in that direction, but the only replies are Grand-mere's standard coded holding signals. She'll know when the timing is right for us to be successful with Merden."

I huffed out a sigh. I didn't like the idea of waiting on timing to correct such evil - in a kingdom I was supposed to be protecting, no less. For all I knew, the attacks on the darkbloods were one hundred percent this bitch vampire's doing.

But I trusted Jai, and I trusted his Grand-mere. As much as I'd learned about Haret, I was still clueless on so much.

"So, what's really worrying you, then? About me going to the pride lands?" There had to be something else. Vampire attacks or not, of all the places I could travel, Sol's sunny home was one of the least threatening.

Jai narrowed his eyes and shook his head. I sensed his mind shuttering up, but not before a single thought slipped out. I hugged him tight, barely able to believe the unspoken fear. I shared it, but I wasn't ready to talk about it, either.

Jai was terrified of adding a helpless child into our unpredictable world.

So terrified that he almost didn't want this quest to

unravel my magical blocks to succeed.

"Oh, Jai," I whispered, pressing my lips to his chest through the thin fabric of his shirt. I felt his heart beating wildly beneath his cool skin, and I felt his pain in being found out.

"I'm sorry, *aima*. It's selfish of me. I would let anyone else in the world suffer before I'd let you. And if there was a child…" His voice broke and he tilted his face up to the wood-beamed ceiling.

"That doesn't make you selfish, Jai. It makes you my *aima*. And it would make you a perfect father," I added, feeling a little shy.

"The sort of father who drives everyone crazy with worry," he grumbled, and I snickered as the mood lightened a bit. Yeah, my vampire would definitely be the kind of dad to lock his daughter up and threaten anyone who showed interest in her with a slow death.

But that was something we could handle when - *if* - we got there.

"I agree with Sol that you should keep out of the pride lands for this one," I told him, and he groaned. He was nodding, though, when a brief knock sounded on the library door.

Dair pushed it open before we'd had a chance to answer, and his face was tight with annoyance.

"Sol?" I asked, starting toward the door, but Dair held up a hand to stop me.

"A summons," he said, holding up a rolled piece of parchment. "The Council wants all three of us in Patriam to discuss the Oracle's death."

"Absolutely not," Jai spit out. "They do not order their Queen anywhere. Go if you wish, but the rest of us will not play their games. Carlyle, continue your plans with Sol. Perhaps this is a good time for me to help Toro investigate his discovery."

Dair nodded. "That sounds reasonable. I've been promising Mother I'd come help smooth things over about the darkbloods, as well."

I nodded. I wanted no part of another Council interrogation. "I'll take Jack and Killian, too, if you think the lions will be okay with them?"

"Let Sol decide," Jai said, a bit of humor crinkling his eyes. "I guess I owe him an apology."

"Yeah, you do," I said, laughing. I didn't like it when we argued - there were already too many people against us for us to give each other any trouble.

CHAPTER TWO

CARLYLE

"So, you're gonna get my vampire all wet?" I teased Toro, while he watched me pack a few things into a backpack. We'd spent the previous day making arrangements to travel to the pride lands, but we were keeping it light this time.

And siphoning, if I had my way. Of all people, the Queen of Haret should get a travel exemption for siphoning.

"Since I can't have you in my air bubble, guess I might as well," Toro said, rolling his eyes and settling on the edge of my bed. It wasn't like my fish not to appreciate a good pun.

"Hey. What's wrong?" I asked, ducking down to see his eyes better.

He shrugged, so I stopped packing and draped myself in his lap. I kissed my way up his neck, nibbling on his full lips. Toro's hands locked around my waist, his long fingers stretching low on my hips.

"Just a little jealous, I guess," he murmured against my kisses. "You haven't even been home from Paris a full week."

I wriggled around so I was straddling his thighs. "I swear, next quest is yours."

He laughed, stroking up my spine and pulling a shiver of anticipation from me. "I don't need a quest. I just want my girl."

"Well, that's no problem. All you had to do was ask." I felt bad that he'd even *had* to ask, but there wasn't much to be done about the fact that Toro's watery discovery couldn't be left unattended, and I needed to keep solving this puzzle.

But that didn't mean we had to rush to be apart.

I pressed myself tighter against Toro, my nipples hard against his chest. "We have on way too many clothes for what I'm about to do," I noted, and he grinned.

"What my lady wants, my lady gets," he said, shucking off his shirt as I did the same. "Mmm, yeah, girl," he added, appreciating the turquoise mesh bra beneath. I'd never been much of a lingerie girl, but a few of my guys appreciated it too much not to keep it in my toolbox.

Toro rolled me under him, sucking my nipple between his teeth right through the fabric. I moaned and writhed beneath him, as he pinned my arms to the bed.

He trailed his hot tongue between my breasts and along my stomach, stopping to kiss gently at my core above my leggings.

"Stay still," he warned, letting go of my arms to tug down my pants and underwear.

Of course, I didn't listen - only Dair had ever been able to convince me that waiting was better. With the rest of my men, I was as impatient as a kid at Christmas. I was off the bed in a flash, flipping Toro on his back with my extra bit of strength and yanking down his shorts.

Giving him a taste of his own medicine, I pinned his arms and mouthed the tip of his cock, which was straining toward me.

"Oh, no, you don't," he said, ending on a groan as I took him deep in my throat. "Come here."

He twisted away from me, only to lunge for my arms and legs. We wrestled a few minutes, but before I knew it, he'd strung me along his body, my back pressed tight against his chest. I was giggling and breathless as his thighs opened mine, and he hooked a knee over my leg to keep me spread wide. One of his strong arms banded around my waist, locking my arms to my sides, and the other slid roughly down my side, slicking through my folds.

"Right where I want you," he whispered in my ear,

rolling onto his side and bowing his back just enough to free his cock from between us. It bounced onto my thigh, the tip pressed against my opening.

"I'll let you believe you made this happen," I teased. We both knew I could flip him again if I got bored, so he got to work proving that wasn't going to be an issue.

Toro's muscles bunched and rolled behind me as he worked to find the perfect angle.

"Oh, hell yes," I moaned as he hit that special spot deep inside. From there, my mer turned on his own special brand of duality. His cock slammed into me hard and fast from behind, his impressive abs powering each movement. His free hand stroked lazy circles around my clit, never giving me quite the pressure I wanted.

Of course, he wanted me to beg.

I wanted him to suffer a little first, though. I knew he wouldn't want to come before me, so I worked my inner muscles to squeeze his cock every time he tried to draw away from me. His breathing began to stutter, and his pace slipped a bit, getting sloppy.

"Not fair, Qilin," he gasped as I popped my ass a bit more, swiveling my hips as much as his grip allowed.

"Fair was never the plan," I replied, grinning as his fingers sped up on my clit, rubbing me hard enough that I forgot all about my games. Soon, I was shaking and moaning as a delicious orgasm rolled through me, washing my whole body with heat.

Toro was only seconds behind, groaning his release as he ground deep inside me. His hands drifted up to squeeze my breasts, rolling my nipples as we both worked to catch our breath.

"The fuck?" Toro whispered, brushing one hand along my arm and tugging at a strand of my hair.

"What's that?" I murmured, my eyes still rolled back in my head.

"Nah, never mind. I think that fucking fucked up my eyes. But maybe now you won't forget about me," Toro whispered in my ear, stroking his fingers up my neck and twisting my head enough for a deep kiss.

"Not a chance, fish. You know you're my keeper. And as soon as you and Jai clear the water, I want to see your discovery. That's my little mermaid grotto, right?"

He laughed, releasing me and rolling onto his back. I twisted around and propped up on an elbow to look at him. His smile wasn't fully formed, though, and there was worry in his deep brown eyes.

"I need Jai down there with me, Qilin. He was right not to let you explore. Something's just not right about that water."

I frowned. "Well, whatever it is, we'll deal with it like we always do. *Together.* As soon as I get back from the pride lands," I added, sighing. I knew I could put off my quest to see Iaga's temple without any drama, but my intuition was bugging the crap out of me. I'd learned the hard way what happened when I ignored my inner guidance system, and I was in no mood to add anything else to our plate.

The sound of someone clearing their throat came from the doorway, and I looked up to see Jack, adorably red-cheeked, staring in at us.

"Jai told me to see if you're, ah, ready?" His voice went up at the end in question, and I smirked at my dragon. He didn't mind sharing in the moment, but every time he caught me in bed with one of my mates, it always seemed to catch him off guard.

"Just about. Let me take a quick shower," I said, winking at Toro. "Oh, did Sol say anything about if Killian is okay to come?"

Jack nodded. "The fae won't have it any other way, and he said he can glamor his way in if things are sticky."

"Good. I wish you could come, too," I said, looking back at Toro as I slid off the bed.

"Nah. There's too little water out there - makes my tail twitch. I'm good here, Qilin." His smile was genuine this time, and I relaxed, knowing my mates would all be happy enough with the mission assignments. Well, as happy as Dair could get visiting his mother in Patriam.

I owed him one, for sure.

The guys cleared out while I did a super-fast shower and collected the rest of what I'd need. Everyone was gathered in the throne room again when I made my way there. I said a quick goodbye to Dair, and he siphoned away immediately, that same look of annoyance plain on his handsome face.

"Take care of my vampire," I warned Toro, giggling when Jai rolled his eyes at me. I turned to Sol, who seemed to have gotten over his bit of temper with the boss, and I raised my eyebrow in challenge.

"I want to siphon there."

He shook his head, but he was smiling. "I figured as much. If anyone could get away with it, it should be you."

"Exactly!" I was glad he saw it my way - or at least wasn't going to stop me. "How about I siphon you first - not right inside, but something farther out. Like that first ridge, where Lata found us," I suggested. "I'll come back here for Jack and Killian and wait a few minutes so you can find your mom and get her mentally prepared for me." I laughed, but it wasn't exactly a joke.

Reina Jazira was in the mid-range of my mothers-in-law - she tolerated me, but I wasn't exactly her favorite.

Sol agreed, and as it turned out, my plan worked perfectly.

When I arrived back in the sunny grass with Jack and Killian in tow, Lata was already there, talking with Sol in low voices as her female guards paced restlessly several yards away.

"Mommy Dearest isn't home right now," Lata called to me, punching Sol lightly on the arm.

"How disappointing," I said under my breath. Lata snickered, because of course she'd heard me.

"Lion ears, Qilin," she said, cupping her fingers

around her ears. "But I understand. My mom is a bit much. She's actually off visiting your kind," she added, gesturing to Jack. "Trying to make some sort of alliance where the dragons will periodically do a fly-over and scan our borders for vampire attacks."

Sol growled something I couldn't catch, and Killian ambled over to rest a hand on his friend's shoulder.

"Wonder what's in it for the dragons?" Jack muttered, but Lata didn't reply.

"So, Sol tells me you're here to visit the temple, but I hope you'll stay for dinner. We could use a new topic of conversation." Her face darkened as she glanced back at her guards. "Everyone is a bit on edge, as you can imagine."

"There haven't been any attacks here," Sol told me quickly, but I saw the fear in his eyes. He was worried about his people, and while I knew we'd told Jai that Merden could wait, I wondered at what cost.

"I'm glad to hear it," I told Lata. "But please, let me know if you think there's something I could be doing to help."

"Well, from what Sol's told me, you have plenty of problems right now. Besides, we shifters have been fending for ourselves for a while now. The whole time the Path was closed, there weren't many Haretians taking our side."

I winced reflexively, and she hurried to apologize.

"I mean, I think we'll be just fine. I think there are more to these riddles than just you having babies. My gut is telling me Haret has some growing to do, too. Now, let's get you to that temple."

I smiled at Sol's younger sister, again appreciating how she seemed both childlike and incredibly mature all at once. She linked her arm through mine, and we led the way through the sweet-smelling waist-high grasses, toward the temple where I'd first met Iaga.

CHAPTER THREE

CARLYLE

Something about the temple was different, but I couldn't quite put my finger on it. I looked back at Sol, sending him the question in his mind. He wandered around the structure, while Jack and Lata spread out to do the same.

"I don't see anything to be concerned about, shortcake," Sol murmured, gesturing to Killian. My fae had been scanning the temple, looking for glamor, but after a minute, he also shrugged.

Nobody except me seemed to be finding anything odd. That meant I could be imagining it. Or maybe it was something to do with Iaga.

I stepped up to the low table in the center and eyed the gap beneath, where the dark earth waited. The others lined the edges of the open-walled temple, watching me. It was way too fucking quiet.

Why was I so nervous? I'd talked with Iaga dozens of times.

I knelt down and shimmied into the table's opening, grimacing at how tomb-like the whole experience still was. Soon, I was on my back, feet deep in the earth, my head barely brushing sunlight.

"Iaga?" I whispered. The air vibrated slightly around me, sort of like a pounding heartbeat or footsteps coming closer. Iaga had never sounded like that. She was more like a swirl of air and misty light.

And she still hadn't answered me.

My forehead began to ache, around the spot where my horn would be if shifted. I was feeling the itchy urge to shift, actually, and there was definitely not enough room here. It was as though some magic were calling to my Qilin, trying to coax her out to play.

Or maybe to fight?

That thought sent a burst of adrenaline through me, and I shoved back into the packed dirt beneath me, scrambling to push myself out of the hole. My feet and fingers skidded against loose soil, though, and I remembered the magiquake I'd inadvertently caused when I first arrived in Haret.

Was it suddenly darker in here? My body froze as I remembered the darkness spilling out of the ground like black blood, and the earth around the fissures smoking and singed from the acidity of the dark magic.

The air in the temple shimmered with heat and the sensation of vibration surrounded my muscles. I tensed and waited, trying not to cramp up.

Then words began to fill my mind. It wasn't exactly a voice like I heard when I spoke with my mates in my head, or even Iaga. It was deep and rich, but lacking emotion. Like an idea that flows to you in meditation.

I am the dark red lifeblood that runs beneath the rivers of Haret. I am the indigo ink of the night sky, and the smoky shadows cast by those of greatness…and everyone else.

I gulped, my skin tingling with the phantom memory of the blistering burn on my skin, from where the darkness had once spilled out of the ground and barely touched me. After speaking so much with Iaga, I'd never felt comfortable with the explanation that she'd caused that pain.

Going on instinct as usual, I addressed the odd echoes as though I could see an entity here. "Are you a goddess too? Or a god? Like Iaga?" She'd never mentioned a counterpart, but hell, Haret always had been chock-full of secrets.

The voice vibrated in my chest. *I need no body. I need no magic. I am simply the darkness that rests inside you. Inside everyone. Yours to deny, or yours to use.*

"Use for balance?" I guessed, hoping I was putting the pieces together correctly. I was still confused as crap, but whatever this was didn't feel threatening any more. The more time I spent soaking in its essence, the more familiar it felt.

Yes, this was the darkness I'd known my whole life.

This was the same darkness I used to take from customers at the summer fairs on Earth, cordoning off my mind so I didn't get saturated with it. The same darkness I used to ward off by eating pints of ice cream and cone after cone of cotton candy.

To balance, the voice confirmed, and a sense of calm washed over me. I could figure this out. It wasn't another enemy to battle.

It was the age-old act we all struggle with - learning to use what power we have for good and not evil. Choosing love instead of fear.

As soon as I thought of love, the darkness seemed to calm and settle, seeping back into the earth around me. I breathed deeply, conscious again of the shaft of sunlight at my crown and the rich darkness at my soles.

Somewhere in the middle of my body, the two met and mingled, and I imagined weighting them both equally. Lifeblood and night sky and shadows weren't evil, and neither was Haret.

Neither were the darkbloods in my kingdom.

I just needed to learn to balance their needs and fears with those of the lightbloods. The darkbloods were my underdog warriors - I could identify with that better than many. Better than most of my mates, actually.

I was about to crawl out of the ground, content with my lesson, when another familiar force slipped in. Dust swirled around me in the tight space, and I sneezed.

"Qilin." This voice was more than familiar - it was a relief to hear Iaga again. She sounded so tired, though. Her voice was soft and so weak.

"Iaga. I hoped to find you here. Are you dying? I thought we saved Haret," I blurted out, real sadness spilling out of me at the thought of losing her.

"Haret is safer than before, thanks to you. But yes, my spirit is returning to the light. Soon I'll simply be part of what makes up a lightblood, just as the darkness you just experienced is part of what makes a darkblood. You have much to learn, Qilin. But don't worry - you don't need to learn it all from me."

"I guess I thought you were immortal," I confessed, feeling like a kid learning Santa wasn't real. Even when she'd told me otherwise, I'd pretended that she would always be there for me. "I thought you *were* Haret, and by saving it, we saved you."

A soft chuckle reached my ears. "*Lots* of them think I'm the spirit of Haret, Carlyle. That the world itself could be contained in a single body like mine. But I don't contain Haret any more than a mother contains her children. I'm just a guide - an intermediary."

"For what? Is there a higher consciousness you answer to?" I felt like I was completely out of my league again. The planet itself had a spirit - which I, too, had thought was Iaga. On one hand, though, it was reassuring. Since I was slated to replace her, I wasn't too keen on the idea of *becoming* Haret, either.

I had a pretty long bucket list still - I had no business becoming a freaking *planet*.

"Silly Haretians…don't understand their own gods any more than humans do."

That didn't really answer my question, but she grew silent. I waited a few minutes, weighing the hundred questions I had left. It felt like I'd only have time for a few more.

"So, are people supposed to be like, worshiping me here now? At temples like this?" This idea bothered me more than most, so I wasn't surprised when it fell out of my mouth.

"No, that comes later. When you're practically legend. When your children's children's children are running around and all that."

I startled at her mention of children. One of my other burning questions. "I'll have them, then. Children."

"Of course. If you want them, you'll have them. And I sense that you want them, even if you're terrified of the idea."

I nodded, admitting it to her as much as to myself. The idea of children as a general concept wasn't very appealing. But imagining a child with Jack's puppy playfulness or Sol's quiet confidence? Or any of the traits I loved so much in my mates? Those thoughts warmed my heart and made it feel possible and a hell of a lot of fun.

"Let them worship how they like for now. Heal the balance by working with the darkness, Carlyle. You've worked with the light enough - that skill will never leave you now. Pull the kingdoms into balance, and your body will balance enough for a child to form."

"How in the two worlds am I supposed to balance these kingdoms?" I said, desperation sweeping through me as I thought of all the problems in Saori Sang, the mystery in Aralia, the constantly deadlocked Council, the shifter attacks, the rebelling darkbloods, the Oracle's murder…the list went on, spilling into my brain like water over a broken dam.

"You don't have to *fix* the kingdoms to balance them," Iaga replied, and the whisper was so faint I almost missed it in my panic. "Go dark, and you'll find the light."

"What? What does that mean?" I cried, recognizing it as a key piece of perfectly confusing advice.

"Go dark to go light," her voice echoed, fading away completely at the last word.

I called to her again and again, both out loud and in my mind, but there was no further reply. I felt like screaming. What did that mean, and why had Iaga lost so much magic and presence since I'd last seen her? Had my rise to power completely drained her?

Was it just her time?

I feared I'd lost another friend, and one of the best

leads we'd ever had in solving puzzles like the one we were currently facing.

I feared I'd never speak to her again, and that made me just fucking *sad*.

Several silent moments passed as I blinked away tears and collected myself, then I pushed slowly against the dirt. This time it pushed back, and I crawled easily out from under the table. I stumbled to my feet and sneezed, blinking in the harsh sunlight.

My eyes finally focused enough to see my three mates and Lata, still surrounding the temple.

They looked haggard, though, as if they'd fought a battle while I'd been underground.

"What is it?" I asked, staring at Sol.

He shook his head, pointing to the ground. I gasped as I saw the torched streaks of stone under my feet, emanating from the temple's table. The bubbling fissures of darkness ripple outward from the temple, searing the grass a dozen yards out. Maybe farther.

Ah, shit.

"We thought ya were gone, Savage," Killian choked out, and I ran to him. He crushed me in his arms, and I caught a whiff of the shock and fear they must have experienced when they witnessed the darkness bubbling up from the temple's tomb.

"Damn, Qilin. Way to raise yourself from the dead. Not even a scratch on you." Lata's voice was light, but it sounded artificial, as if she were trying way too hard to brush off what had just happened.

"I'm sorry, guys. I had no idea…I'm okay, though.

It didn't hurt me at all," I rambled, trying to reassure them.

"I took to the sky to check it out. It looks like a dark sun," Jack added, gesturing at the rough circle of dark lines surrounding us. "And, baby? There was another dragon in the distance."

I frowned at him, uncertain what meaning that might have.

"Uh oh," Lata whispered, and I snapped my attention to where she was staring. Well, crap. Reina Jazira had evidently made it back in time to witness me spilling darkness into her home.

Again.

The matriarch of the lion shifters strode toward us with rage on her face. A subtle growl vibrated in her throat, and I swallowed hard. Damn it, I'd been hoping not to piss off another relative today.

"With all due respect to your endorsement by our beloved goddess Iaga, I request that you leave my land, Qilin Queen!" Jazira practically spat the title back at me, throwing it in my face that I was still a fumbling idiot, in her opinion.

"Mother, it's not-"

Sol's words were cut off by a flick of her fingers. He pressed his lips together and narrowed his eyes, but he stayed silent.

"Reina Jazira, I sincerely apologize. I didn't know the darkness would spill out like this, of course. I only meant to speak with Iaga. She is very weak, and I thought the temple where we first spoke might hold some extra power." It sounded dumb as I spoke it out loud to the furious lioness, but I needed to trust my own instincts.

They had been the only things I had to trust, most of my life.

"I don't care about your intentions. I only see my land in danger again, because of your presence." Her face softened for just a moment as she looked at Sol and Lata. "I have to protect what's mine, as well."

"I understand. Was anyone hurt?"

She shook her head. "The magiquake doesn't seem to have reached any of the village. But our temple is destroyed. Nobody will come here to worship now."

I glanced around, wondering if I should try to explain that worship wasn't even necessary. Probably not the right time.

"I'm very sorry. Please let me know how I can help," I said again.

"Please just leave our land. In the future, perhaps we can meet on neutral ground." She smiled tightly, and I relaxed in relief. She wasn't totally writing me off - she was just worried about her people. I could totally relate to that.

"Iaga has tasked me with balancing the darkness and the light. I'm sorry again - I know I'll make mistakes along the way. But please know I have only the good of Haret and all its citizens in my heart."

Jazira sighed and nodded, the last of her anger deflating. "I know, Qilin. I know."

With that, she turned and strode back toward the

village.

Lata watched her go, her lips pursed in thought. Sol and Jack crowded around me as though double-checking that I was really fine.

"Now what, shortcake? Did you learn what you needed?" Sol asked, cupping his fingers under my chin and pulling my face up to look into my eyes.

I snorted. "Sort of. I mean, I have more understanding, but no idea what step to take next."

"I might have an idea," Lata said, stepping over a line of smoking darkness to reach us. "But it's just a hunch, and it's fairly dangerous."

I laughed, and I caught Killian's grin. "Well, if that doesn't sound like our kind of plan, then I don't know what is."

"Let me send one of my generals back for some food, and we'll hash it out here," she suggested, gesturing toward an unharmed grassy spot in the sun. I nodded - a late-afternoon picnic lunch sounded perfect, actually.

"With some of those shifter cakes, yeah?" Jack called after Lata, giving me a sly wink.

"You know me too well, dragon," I said, grinning at my men.

CHAPTER FOUR

CARLYLE

"Are you sure we're okay to eat here?" I asked, watching as Lata unpacked the food. My mouth was already watering, but even though we'd moved pretty far beyond the temple, I wanted to respect Jazira's request for us to leave.

"She won't run us away for eating," Sol answered with a confidence I totally didn't share.

"Guys, I'm so sorry," Lata repeated for the millionth time, but I waved her words away again. There was no reason for her to apologize for her mother. To be honest, if someone came along and fucked up the woods around my castle like this, I'd probably act the same way.

"So, what's your idea?" I asked Lata as we all settled in the grass.

"I was going to bring this up after I talked to Mom, but now, I think it's just better that I tell you. Then you guys can decide if it's worth it or not, because it doesn't really concern her that much. And it might be nothing-"

"Lata. What is it?" Sol cut his sister's rambling off with an impatient motion.

She took a deep breath and lowered her voice even more, although we were the only ones in the flower-dotted field. "I started thinking about it when you guys mentioned the heartstone and the singing stone. Sol, remember the old stories of moonstone mines in the southern rain forests beyond our land?"

Sol nodded, looking confused. "Those were never confirmed, though."

"Well, a family of midnight jaguars has been spotted in and around that area, and the rumors are starting again. I just thought…maybe a moonstone could help. I mean, I don't know much about *sruth*, but the moons balance the darkness of night. Maybe a moonstone could…I don't know. It's probably a stupid idea."

Sol patted his sister awkwardly on the shoulder, but I tilted my head, considering the idea. It felt right, even if I couldn't explain why. I'd hoped Iaga would give me explicit answers, but maybe what she'd given me was fortification to simply trust myself.

"I need to stop looking to everyone else for answers," I mumbled, and Lata slumped. "No, I don't mean you! I actually really like your idea. I just meant we've been reading ancient books and consulting doctors and oracles and temples. I think it's time for me to stop searching for answers that are already inside of me."

"I like the way that sounds, baby," Jack said, wrapping his arm around my shoulders and kissing my cheek.

"Jaguars are the worst kind of cat shifters," Killian warned, his tone sharp. "They double-cross as much as the fae, and they're as fierce as the vampires. Fuckin' smart, too, and nearly always darkblood."

"I'd say a lot of that makes them pretty good shifters," I shot back, and he had the decency to flush. "Maybe even the kind we need on our side."

Sol frowned. "I don't know, shortcake. Killian's not wrong. Our pride has always made a point to get along with the surrounding shifters, but jaguars aren't the type to compromise if they want something."

"But Iaga said go dark to go light," I insisted, latching onto the cryptic idea again. "Jaguars are mostly darkblooded. And midnight coats mean they're literally dark, right? And the forest is dark."

I was totally grasping at straws to explain my gut feeling, and thank fuck my guys didn't call me on it. It was impossible to describe where a hunch came from - like trying to hold sand in your fist.

"Let's do it," Sol agreed, surprising me by being

the first one to agree. "But only if Lata comes - we need your intel and lion senses, little sister."

She grinned a mile wide, while I felt like acting the way Jai usually did. We had no business dragging Sol's sister into this mess, and damned if I didn't want yet another tally against me on Jazira's shit list.

But I took a bit of my own medicine and pushed all my objections away, trusting Sol's intuition too.

"Only if you want to," I cautioned instead, nodding to her.

Lata laughed. "Of course, I fucking want to. My generals can cover my shift - and cover with Mom, if needed."

"We're not telling her, are we?" I asked Sol, unsure which would be better.

"Fuck, no," he replied, a feline glint in his eye that I hadn't seen in a while. The hairs on the back of my neck rose, and I felt blood rush to my cheeks at the sensation.

I loved it when my lion was a sweet kitten, but damn, seeing him get all sly and predatory would be hot as hell, too.

"What gear do we need?" Kills asked.

"Um, lightweight clothes, good boots. Maybe a torch?" Lata guessed. "It's not far. We can be there by nightfall, camp on the outer edge, and head into the jungle at first light?"

"We have all that," Jack said, gesturing to the small packs we'd brought, even though I'd siphoned us in.

"What will they want in exchange for a

moonstone?" I asked as we began to pack up the remaining food to take with us. There was way more than we could have eaten in one meal, and I suspected Lata had requested it that way on purpose. I liked a girl who thought ahead.

If I ever got Kana and her together, the three of us could do some serious ass-kicking.

"There's no telling, but it probably won't be cheap," Sol admitted, a worried look crossing his face. He smoothed it away in an instant, though. "Doesn't matter, though. If they have what you need, we'll get it, shortcake." That feral narrowing of his eyes was back, and it thrilled me even more.

My kitty was going hunting, and I was going to have a hell of a time watching.

We shouldered our packs, and Lata scampered off to tell her generals the plan. It wasn't long before she slid into step beside Sol, though, as he was leading the way.

I was mostly silent at first, mulling over Iaga's words and the revelation of the darkness. I sent tidbits of the intel to my guys as we moved, trying to make sense of it as I did.

"Tell me more about the moonstones," I suggested.

"They're typically pale and iridescent and smooth, like a full moon," Lata began. "Those are pretty easy to find in any market."

Sol continued, "But there's a lot of lore around them, just like the heartstone you ended up with, and the Oracle's soul stone. There are just a few known colored moonstones, and they're rumored to be as powerful as they are rare. Earth has its blood moon and its harvest moon, right? Haret has those sorts of things, too. My favorite has always been the sunrise moon. It's a creamy, soft orange like you see in early morning, and it only happens a couple of times a year."

"That sounds beautiful." I smiled at Sol, hoping one day I'd get to see the sunrise moon with him here in Haret - maybe even in the pride lands.

Lata walked backward effortlessly, adding, "Legend says that a moonstone mined under the light of a sunrise moon will have crazy-strong healing properties. So that's what I'm hoping to find with the jaguars."

Her eyes looked so hopeful and excited that I had to grin back.

Crazy-strong healing sounded like just the thing my *sruth* - and Haret - needed. And if some darkbloods helped me get it, even better.

I felt a twinge of guilt at not updating Jai with the new plan, but I knew he'd come rushing in. And if the vampire attacks were as serious as we'd been told, that was the last thing we needed.

Surely, he and Toro were having at least a little fun back at the castle, exploring Toro's "water under the water", as he'd called it.

I smiled to myself as we headed over a final crest, and I saw the deep green top of the rain forest spreading before us in the distance.

CHAPTER FIVE

TORO

I could tell Jai was on edge, thinking about Carlyle being gone from the castle. Can't say it made me feel great, either, but I'd made up my mind a long time ago that our girl was going to do what our girl was going to do.

And I was proud of her for it, too.

"What exactly makes you think there's something worth investigating beneath the pool you dug?" Jai asked, his tone curious as he stared into the blue-tinged depths of the grotto pool.

He hadn't been in the water at all since we'd found the lower level - none of them had, actually. Except

Carlyle, for that one hot moment before she left for Paris. I was patiently waiting for my turn to take her somewhere special, but I didn't exactly mind being the one she gave her best goodbyes to.

I studied the water, trying to figure out how to describe my gut feeling. "Part of it's a mer thing, probably. You know, sensing the temperature and vibration of the water. There's a current down there that's really fucking different from what we've filled the pool with. It's deep, though. There are plenty of caves and tunnels, too. And every time I dive down to check it out, it moves a bit, like it's not interested in being found."

Jai snorted. "That's ridiculous. Water doesn't have sentience. Are you suggesting there's something living down there? Maybe something using magic to cover itself?"

I shrugged. There could be a dozen explanations for what I was feeling. With all the shit we'd been through in the past years, though, I just wanted someone strong with me to really check it out. Carlyle would have been perfect, with her mer shift and rainbow of magic.

But the vampire would have to do - none of the team was going to consent to our girl being the canary in the coal mine.

"Let's go, then," Jai growled, shucking off his shirt and toeing off his boots.

I pulled up the magic that would let him breathe underwater, and we both grabbed some waterproof torches Dair had spelled before blinking away to Patriam. Both of us had some decent vision in darkness, but water didn't cooperate the same way as air.

Once we were below the grotto's pool, there wouldn't be any natural light source.

I dove into the pool and shifted instantly, Jai splashing in behind me. The corner we'd dug deep into was on the southern edge of the grotto, and the water was cool around me, like swimming through the shadowy edges of a lake.

Pointing at the fissure in the floor of the pool, I guided Jai toward the place where we could squeeze through. That was the other reason I was wary - that opening seemed to be widening even though we'd stopped digging immediately after finding it.

Side by side, we swam deeper into the cavern beneath the castle's foundation. We were completely underwater - no air pockets anywhere I could tell. I'd explored quite a bit on my own, but I still hadn't found the source for this aquifer.

As we swam past the point where I'd stopped exploring before, I noticed the slightly sour taste of salt water. I motioned to Jai, and he nodded. He'd noticed it, too.

Even though we were hundreds of miles from the coast, this must link up with the ocean somewhere. Haret was full of underground tributaries, but I'd never seen one this far inland.

Jai slowed and held his torch up to the side of the

cave we were in, running his palms over the smooth rock wall. In my mind, he asked, *Does this look man-made? Is it possible this was created, like you've been digging the grotto?*

I examined the place he was pointing to, but I could only shrug. I answered, *It's possible some of this was carved by hand, but I doubt the whole thing was. It's just too massive. That's what makes me wonder how much Iaga even knew about this castle. For all we know, she might have inherited it like we did.*

Jai nodded, exploring farther. We both kept the torches extended - it was like swimming through the night sky. There were a few bio-luminescent creatures and some streaks on the cave walls, but the water was mostly still and black.

Of course, growing up in the ocean, I knew how easy it was for someone to spy on you, shrinking into the reef or beneath the sand. Or like here, behind the rock formations.

The deeper we explored, the surer I was that something really was down here, watching us. Toying with us, to be exact.

I feel it, too. There's a carefully guarded mind down here, Jai admitted when I asked him about it.

We'd gone deep and far enough that I was starting to worry we'd lose our way home, when I finally saw a flicker of movement. Something big enough to make the water ripple toward us as it swam away.

Jai and I whirled back-to-back, swimming in a rough circle and scanning the area with our torches. It took a hell of a lot for the boss to get afraid, but I felt the quickening of his heart through the water's connection.

Whatever was stalking us would definitely feel it, too.

Then my torch caught the glint of eyes in the darkest corner of the tunnel ahead, and I broke formation to chase it down. It rushed me, tumbling me head over fin, and headed straight for Jai.

I righted myself in time to see Jai swinging wildly with his torch at the mass of darkness swirling around him. He wasn't using his ice magic, though, and I wondered if he was holding back to test its abilities.

There was a vague person shape to it, but the layers of shadows made it nearly impossible to tell much.

I dove into the mess, colliding with something very real - and as icy cold as Jai's skin could get when his eyes went pure black.

The water vibrated with something like a shriek, and my ears ached with pulsing pain.

I yanked Jai's arm, guiding us back down the tunnel we'd entered. We swam like hell through the tight spaces, pausing only when we saw the tiny bit of light from the grotto above us. Knowing we were that close was more comforting than I wanted to admit, and we both needed a serious breather.

What the fuck was that? I asked Jai through our mind connection.

I'm not really sure, but I can still sense it following us. We need to get out of here and seal this crack, Jai answered, a bit more fear in his tone than I'd heard in a long time. Whatever this thing was, we couldn't let it get loose in the castle.

We swam hard toward the opening above us, which would lead us back to the grotto. But barely a yard short, the thing flashed in front of us again, the impossible scream shattering my eardrums.

The water roiled around us, currents of ice wrapping my tail and threatening to yank me deep. It was the sort of tricks I'd heard of sea witches using to lure non-mer to their deaths, but with the grotto's extra light unraveling the darkness, I could tell this thing before us was no mer.

It barely had a body, much less a tail.

It was a mass of sinuous darkness with flashing teeth and glowing eyes.

Something about it was eerily familiar, but I wasn't about to take the time to study the thing. It hurled some sort of electrical bolt at us through the water, singeing the edge of my fin as I darted out of the way. Whirling, I saw Jai absorb the bulk of it, but his vampire strength seemed to take it in stride.

He surged forward, grabbing at the thing, but it darted to the side easily.

Jai's voice flooded my mind, ordering me up into the pool, and I shot through the narrow opening. Several of my scales were scraped off in the ascent, but I made it into the warmer water just seconds before he scrambled through the opening.

I darted toward the pile of rocks Sol had hauled up from our digging and toppled several of the large ones back over the edge into the water. Jai shoved them in place to block the opening.

Darkness leaked into the grotto's clearer water like ink from an octopus, but the creature didn't come into the pool

I wasn't convinced our quick fix was actually holding it back, though. I floated near the surface of the pool, watching as the shadows dissipated, dissolving back into the water. A pair of white eyes gleamed at me through a gap in the rocks, though, and I shivered despite myself.

Whatever it was, that thing was creepy as fuck.

We surfaced, and Jai ripped open the air bubble himself rather than wait for me to pull back my magic.

"Have you seen a sea creature anything like that before?" he demanded, hauling himself onto the edge of the pool. He was breathing hard.

I flopped onto the stone floor and shifted, not really wanting to be in the water. I shook my head, still somewhat dazed. "My guess is it's fae - not mer."

"What makes you think that?" Jai demanded, but I had little evidence to go on.

"A gut feeling, I guess. But it didn't have any sort of mer body. And the magic isn't like ours, either. It was more like fae magic," I ended lamely. There were probably other creatures the thing could be, too.

"You were with her before she left, right?" Jai

asked, and I blinked at him, my brain trying to catch up and understand his question. "Carlyle. You had sex with her," he explained dryly.

"Uh, yeah. In her room," I answered, frowning. Where the hell was he going with this?

"Did you see anything - anything like that darkness - when you were fucking?"

My eyes widened. "Holy shit," I whispered. The odd sense of familiarity clicked into place with his question. The darkness, the flashing eyes and teeth. "Holy shit. Yeah. Carlyle seemed to flash dark like that thing for a second. The eyes…" I trailed away, remembering how Carlyle's eyes had flashed white like that. My stomach turned.

"I've seen it, too. In Paris," Jai admitted. "I thought it was my eyes playing tricks in the sun, or maybe a bit of glamor she let slip. But I can't erase that sense of similarity. But what the fuck would cause it? And when did it start?"

I shook my head at the impossible questions.

Really, I just didn't want to think of the implications. Had our girl somehow been magicked by this thing? I mean, she *had* been in the water with me before Jai took her to Paris. Was part of it clinging to her like a parasite?

Ugh, the thought creeped me out big time.

"It's not her," Jai growled, and I felt his mind brushing against mine. "Whatever this thing is, we must never let it affect our actions toward Carlyle."

I nodded, needing no such order. It would break

our Qilin's heart to think any of us were afraid of her the way I felt about this monster in our water. Probably piss her the hell off, too.

"We need to figure this shit out before she gets home," I said, realizing how impossible that might be even as the words slipped out.

Jai didn't answer, only stared grimly toward the southern corner of the pool, as though he were waiting for the dark creature to slip through and steal the greatest happiness we all had.

CHAPTER SIX

CARLYLE

We'd reached the edges of the rain forest just as darkness was falling, and we'd quickly eaten and made camp about a half mile from the actual jungle. Sol and Lata claimed this was far enough to keep us out of trouble with any guards, but we still split the night into watch rotations.

I had done mine first, hoping to get an uninterrupted rest afterward. Of course, now I couldn't sleep, no matter what I tried.

I sighed at Lata's still form across the dying embers - she'd passed out so easily after her shift. Even Sol was breathing evenly, snuggled up behind me by the fire, his hand wrapping my waist. I sensed Jack gliding above me in the night air, and I almost shifted to join him. But no - I needed to sleep, damn it.

I bit down on another sigh, and my lion stirred, cinching me tighter against him. I tried to sink into his warmth and willed my mind to stop churning.

"Are you worried? About going into the rain forest?" Sol asked drowsily, his breath warm on my cheek. His hand grazed my neck as he swept my hair back. A delicious shiver slunk up my spine as his lips dropped to my throat, his curls tickling my skin. "I know you haven't been sleeping."

I wriggled my ass a little against him, a new thought raising its hand for consideration. Maybe I could burn off my nervous energy some other way.

"I mean…if you're up, I guess I could use a distraction," I suggested, arching my neck and back at the same time. His mouth opened against my skin, and his tongue scraped up the side of my neck. I felt his cock hardening quickly behind me, pressed tight against my lower back.

Yeah, this was better. If I couldn't have sleep, I'd at least have sugar.

"I'm up for you," he rasped, his palm slipping lower on my stomach. The tips of his fingers grazed beneath the waist of my pants. "But really - do you have any hesitation about tomorrow?"

I paused my lustful thoughts long enough to truly consider his question. I was feeling restless, but in my heart, I knew it wasn't the jaguars. "No, I don't think I do. It's hard to explain, but I trust my gut on this one - and Lata's."

"Good. That means I can put all my attention elsewhere."

"I like that plan, too," I said, twisting just enough to meet his mouth with mine. Our kiss was slow and lazy, like we had all the time in the world. His hand pinched the skin at my waist, though, and I could taste his impatience even if he was trying his best to be a gentleman and control it.

It had been a hot minute since I'd had my lion.

"You know," I murmured around his lips. "I caught a bit of that ferocity in your eyes earlier, and I kinda liked it. I know you play hard and fast with Kills sometimes," I added, grinning at how he tensed up.

"I do," he admitted. "And he likes it."

"I like it sometimes, too," I returned, arching an eyebrow. Sol had always been about me and my pleasure, but I enjoyed taking my men to the edge on occasion. It was a certain type of pleasure to feel totally used by someone for their own needs, and I was in the mood for something a little rough and dirty.

"Throw up a bit of that soundproofing, then, shortcake," Sol said, his voice a rumbly challenge.

I smirked at him. "Gonna make me scream?" His answering grin yanked an ache from deep in my core, and I tugged the invisible barrier over us like a blanket. Sol lifted up to brace his arms on either side of mine, pinning me between his muscles.

One of his hands slid up my stomach under my thin shirt, his fingers twisting the fabric. A few claws shifted out, and the shirt shredded just enough for him to yank it off, baring me in an instant. I gasped, and a giggle escaped my parted lips.

His palm slid between my breasts, claws just barely scraping the sensitive skin before his long fingers closed loosely around my neck.

"So, you want me to fuck you on the rough side tonight?" His words vibrated through me, sending a pulse of desire from the fingers locked on my jugular, straight to my core.

"I want you to show me your dominant side," I taunted, shoving at his chest a little. He gazed down at me as if deciding what direction to take. His fingers tightened around my throat just enough to make me feel it, and he lowered his lips to my bare breasts.

Sol alternated between gentle licks and nips on both breasts, keeping an opposite rhythm with the loosening and tightening of his fingers along the sides of my neck.

I tilted my chin up and gave into the sensations, losing myself in the pale glow of Haret's moons above us.

Thinking of the sunrise moon, I wondered how it would look if one was pale orange. I conjured up a tendril of Sol's orange magic and wafted it in the sky just above me, obscuring the pale face of one of the moons.

"Pay attention," Sol growled as he nipped me hard, catching on that I was floating instead of focusing.

I opened my mouth to apologize, but he flipped me onto my stomach in one swift, rough movement. The air was pushed from my lungs, and I barely had time to recover when he yanked my pants down, leaving them just under the swell of my ass. The fabric was tight across my hips, keeping my thighs pressed together.

"I hope you're wet for me, shortcake, because if not, it's going to be a rough night."

I moaned as he squeezed my ass with both hands, his fingers definitely tight enough to leave marks. He had nothing to worry about - I was so ready. He wrenched my hips up and pushed my pants down a few inches more, arching my back and spreading me open to the humid night air.

"Goddamn. That ass," he groaned, kneeling behind me and pressing his mouth to my core. He licked a solid line from front to back, trailing his fingers behind. One slipped inside my asshole. "You want me to fuck you here? Or do you want me buried deep in this sweet pussy?" At least two fingers buried themselves deep in my pussy, and I cried out as he pumped me hard both ways.

"I want you everywhere you want to be," I answered, my body pressing back into him in wanton need. His fingers left my body, and he reached forward and grabbed my arms, yanking them behind me. I resisted just enough to make it a struggle, but he soon held both wrists easily in one large hand.

My face was pressed against the blanket, and I turned to rest on one cheek. I could just glimpse him over my shoulder, and fuck, he was hot to watch. His golden hair was loose and waved around his shoulders in a tantalizing hint of his lion form, and he rippled with muscle under his thin shirt.

One-handed, he undid his pants and freed his long cock. It was already straining toward my body, the size of it promising a hell of a ride. His golden skin gleamed in the moonlight, and I wished he were naked so I could see more of it.

I knew Sol could be patient, and I knew he could be gentle. What I hadn't seen as much of was his roughness - unless it was with Killian. I knew he sometimes pinned the fae and took his ass hard and fast, and I was practically salivating imagining him doing the same with me.

"Don't be polite, now. Fuck me, lion," I urged, holding my breath when I felt the tip of his cock nudge against my pussy.

"Take it all, then, and fucking like it," he groaned, shoving into me in one fierce thrust. My body arched hard with the force of his movements, and my face was buried in the blanket.

Sol yanked backward on my arms, keeping me upright in the position he needed. His other hand locked on my hip for leverage, and he began a wild rhythm. Deep, throaty growls vibrated down his chest and abs, hitting me right in the hips as he pounded deep inside me, and I whimpered with the building need.

"Fucking yes," I mumbled, my voice ending on a load moan as he pressed harder on my back, arching me even farther. The angle was both impossible and breathtakingly deep.

I was paralyzed with pleasure and struggling to catch my breath. He let go of my hip and his free hand pinched and rolled my ass, marking me all over as his. I could feel him coming apart a little as he switched it up again, letting go of my wrists.

He yanked my hips against him and ground into me. His thrusts were completely wild now, his growl edging more on a roar as he fucked me harder than he'd ever dared. My body took it all and loved it.

I bit down on my lips, fighting to keep from coming first. I needed to feel him unravel first - I wanted to feel used. I wanted to feel *needed*. It was the headiest sort of power to wield.

SOL

I'd totally lost my mind, fucking her like this.

For some reason, although I knew her body was tougher than mine and healed twice as fast, I'd never quite dared to give her my full lion strength.

Her sweet body quivered around mine, her pale

skin shining in the moonlight. I struggled to hold back my orgasm. It didn't work very long, though, and my lion's roar echoed deep into the rain forest as I came so hard I saw stars behind my eyes.

My body was too ramped up to stop, and I kept pounding into her, anxious to give her something of what I was feeling, at least. My fingers found her clit all on their own, and it was mere seconds before she was screaming out my name for all the world to hear.

We collapsed in a sweaty, exhausted heap on the blanket, and I registered what I'd just realized.

For all the world to hear - ah, fuck. Yeah, she'd dropped the barrier at some point, and the whole camp and rain forest had probably heard what we were up to.

Even - yep. Goddamn it. Lata was sitting up, blinking sleepily at me, her lip curled in a too-much-information expression. Her eyes slid to Carlyle, though, and she actually scrambled backward.

Glancing down at my girl, I nearly did the same.

"What the fuck?" I muttered, my heart pounding for a whole new reason.

The girl I'd just fucked didn't look anything like *my* girl. Her grin was dark and feral, and her skin and hair were silky black. Eyes flashed blinding white and solid, and her teeth snapped sharp and fang-like.

"Carlyle?" I whispered, my voice shaking.

A soft cackle came from the black lips. "Who else would I be?"

I recoiled, though, because the voice was all

fucking wrong. Too low and gravelly - too sinister.

"What the fuck is it, Sol," Lata hissed, pinpointing my unease. This *thing* in front of me was decidedly not my Queen, even though she'd been here a few seconds ago.

CHAPTER SEVEN

CARLYLE

Sol was giving me the weirdest look. Almost like he was afraid of me, but that didn't make sense. He buttoned up his pants in record time and muttered something about checking on Killian and Jack.

My cheeks were flushed with the heady pleasure of our fun, but my heart was feeling a little left out in the cold.

Maybe I was just too used to Sol's standard bedside manner. But then I looked at Lata, and the girl couldn't meet my eyes, either. She was acting super skittish, too.

Ah, shit.

"I let the barrier down, didn't I?" I grumbled, shimmying back into my pants.

I could tell Lata's face went blood red even in the weak moonlight.

"Goddamn it. I'm so sorry, Lata. That must be awkward as hell." I bit my bottom lip, hoping the apology would be enough. I mean, I had no idea what else to do about it.

"It's okay," she mumbled. Her eyes darted toward me again, as though she wanted to say something else.

"What is it?" I asked after a couple minutes of her shifty eyes.

"That…that dark form. It's creepy as shit. Why did you do it?" she asked, sounding like she'd realized she didn't know me at all. Like I'd done something to Sol that she didn't approve of.

I tilted my head. "Dark form?"

"Yeah. The black hair and white eyes and fangs and shit." She gestured at me.

"I have no idea-" My confusion was cut off by a sort of screaming roar from the direction of the rain forest. It definitely wasn't Sol, either.

"Shit! The jaguars!" Lata shot to her feet and shifted, bounding in the direction Sol had gone.

I shook off the uneasy feeling her question had sparked - I had no idea what she was talking about, but it obviously needed to be discussed.

The problem was going to be when, exactly.

"Carlyle!" Jack's voice reached me from over a small hill, and I stumbled to my feet. I tried to smooth my clothes and hair as I hurried to meet him.

"The jaguars have come out to meet us. To ah, tell us to go away, from the sounds of it."

I frowned. Well, that was rude. "Do they know who I am?" I sighed at myself as the question slipped out - was I really going to be that kind of celebrity?

But seriously. I wasn't sure they actually *could* deny me entrance, if I really wanted to go.

It might hurt my rocky relations with the other darkbloods, though.

"Sol is trying to smooth it over now. It seems they ah, felt threatened by the ah, noise. Thought it was some sort of war cry, I guess?"

I muttered a curse under my breath, while trying not to grin at the flush on Jack's cheeks. Hey, a girl had a right to enjoy her mate. But maybe our timing could have been better.

Jack grabbed my hand and tugged me in the direction he'd come from.

As we got closer to the edge of the jungle, I could see Sol and Lata, both shifted back to their person forms, talking with a man too shadowed for me to really see him.

I could see the jaguars, though, as they paced the clearing. Damn, they were gorgeous. All the ones I could see had midnight black coats that were gleaming in the moonlight, and their eyes ranged from glowing yellow to bright turquoise. They were definitely bigger than any jaguar I'd seen on Earth.

I started to walk closer, but Jack held me back.

"They know you're here. Don't get closer yet, though. Sol wanted to talk with them, you know, feline to feline." He chuckled, and I nodded and leaned into him. Hopefully, Sol could calm them down and present our case well.

SOL

These jaguars were making me nine kinds of nervous. Their dark, sinewy forms and the large whites of their eyes reminded me too much of the *thing* that had possessed Carlyle just a few short minutes ago. A glance back at my girl standing next to Jack showed her back to normal, but I couldn't erase that feral grin from my mind.

I could tell Lata was spooked, too, but she was doing a great job explaining why we'd come.

If I didn't know better, I'd be asking the jaguars if they were responsible for Carlyle's dark form. I'd never heard of shifter magic that could do anything like what had happened, though. And Carlyle didn't even seem to know it had happened. Of course, I hadn't exactly paused to ask her if she'd glamored herself into a demon for kicks.

But that just wasn't something my girl would do.

I shook the thoughts away - I needed to focus on what the man before me was saying to Lata.

"You've heard some interesting rumors, little cub.

I wonder which of my brothers is responsible for them?" The man swiveled his head back to glare at the jaguars circling us, and a few of them ducked their heads in deference.

He was slim but muscled like Jai, and dusky skinned, with glossy black curls covering his ears. When I looked at my sister, I caught her studying him with an interest that was a bit more than self-preservation.

"I've heard no rumors directly from jaguars," she clarified. "Perhaps there are others in your jungle?"

He raised an eyebrow at her, considering. "We'll blame it on the birds, then. But why do two such golden, sun-infused lions have such a keen interest in moonstones?"

"Anyone can receive power from the moon," Lata hedged.

"And what of the smoke-scented sky lizard in the distance? And the air fae? Yes, I scent him, too, and he's getting a little too close for his own good. Why have you brought this assortment of companions?"

Lata glanced at me, and I figured it was time to lay our cards on the table. "The dragon and fae are mated to the Qilin Queen. As am I. We're here on her behalf, to request a moonstone."

"And what about you? Are you mated to the new Queen, as well?" he asked Lata, one side of his mouth raising in a smirk to match the eyebrow.

"No, I'm not mated at all," Lata blurted, and I felt my big-brother hackles start to rise when the man's mouth stretched into a full grin.

One of the jaguars nearby made a growly sort of meow, and the one speaking to us nodded.

"We'll take the Queen, and only the Queen, into the jungle with us. The jungle will decide if she gets a moonstone," he said, turning back to me.

"No fucking way," I spat out. Jai would have my ass - this wasn't a matter of whether Carlyle was strong enough. This was fucking disrespectful, and with all our trouble with darkbloods lately, our girl just might find herself in an ambush of epic proportions.

"No deal," affirmed Lata.

"Suit yourself." He shrugged, and of course, we realized the jaguars were holding all the cards. I glanced back to where I knew Carlyle was waiting with Jack, but she only shook her head.

In my mind, she said, *Let's wait until morning and do this more officially. These might not even be the ones in charge.*

"Come on, Lata. Perhaps the Queen can return in the morning and speak with someone besides the night watch," I said, hazarding a guess.

Lata and I turned and walked away, ignoring the growls that told me we'd been right on the money.

CARLYLE

We all trudged back to camp in silence. Sure, I still felt like a dumbass, but I refused to be turned away because of a mistake. It looked like it had just been some uppity guards.

Tomorrow we'd make our plea to someone actually in charge. Surely, that would make a difference, but I recognized I'd need to figure out a benefit for the jaguars. Maybe I could siphon back to the castle and bring them some kind of gift? Of course, that would complicate things, because Jai would certainly insist on coming, and that might spook the jaguars even more...

Killian tugged me down next to him as Sol circled the camp on watch. I snuggled under my blanket, vowing to try and sleep on it - again. Thankfully, my eyes drifted closed in sleep almost immediately, and it didn't take long for dreams to grab hold of my mind.

I dreamed I had taken matters into my own hands, and I was already walking through the dense jungle. Stars peeked through the canopy at random intervals, but very little moonlight made it down to the ground. Leaves crackled beneath my feet as I let my dream body drift.

"Qilin Queen."

I turned toward the welcome voice, so happy to hear from the goddess again, even if it were only a dream.

"You should know this isn't just a dream," Iaga said, her low laughter rustling through the leaves around me.

"I was worried the temple might be the last time I spoke with you," I admitted, realizing I was definitely too aware for this to be a regular dream. Iaga floated into view before me, her body misty and sort of hovering above the jungle floor.

"Learn to trust yourself more, Carlyle. The wisdom I have is from the same places you have access to - the wisdom of all the energy in the universe. Tune into it. You'll make mistakes - you'll hear things wrong. But that's no reason not to listen."

She paused before a mossy slope, brushing aside some fallen leaves and settling into the dirt. I stood before her, waiting for more of her perfect advice. She continued to stare up into the shifting leaves, though, until my patience ran out, and a question popped out.

"I just can't stop worrying about this darkblood thing. What if I can't figure it out in time? What if I make everything worse?"

Iaga smiled, plucking a waxy white flower from a nearby vine and twirling it between her fingers. "You're learning about your *sruth*, right? If we hold negative thoughts like fear and worry inside of us, our *sruth* become soiled with that deep, dense energy. You know what I speak of. You felt it in Jantzen's cane, didn't you?"

I startled, a sudden queasiness sloshing through me as I remembered exactly how it had felt to stab the Ringmaster's cane straight through with my horn.

The pain and the utter wrongness of it still haunted me.

"What happens if I can't get rid of the negativity, though? What if I'm still afraid?" I asked, hating the tremble in my voice. I wasn't sure I could just stop thinking through the cons or the possible negative outcomes of a situation. It seemed almost irresponsible, like everything would collapse if I didn't worry about it.

"The fear will never cease, of course. But you must learn to act *through* it. If you dwell on the fear and worry, eventually, you won't be able to push enough energy through your *sruth* to use your magic. Your goddess powers will dwindle - not unlike mine, though many hundreds of years before your time." Iaga sighed, and her form flickered enough that I could see the vines behind her. "You'll feel out of balance. Your body and mind will be sluggish, as though you walk through water or sand. And you'll lose that wonderful sense of pattern-finding that serves you so well - that's your natural psychic power, my goddess Queen."

"Well, damn," I muttered. It sounded like burn out, and I'd felt it before when I had worked the carnival circuit too many dozens of nights in a row. It was a fucking good reason to figure this out and stop worrying.

"You will," Iaga whispered, proving that even at ten percent power, she could still read my mind. "Now, head back to your body, little Qilin, before trouble finds you."

Her form faded enough that I assumed she'd gone wherever she usually did, but I felt comforted by our conversation.

I was on the right track, then, with the stones. I knew they cleansed chakra - *sruth* - I just had to find more of them without killing anyone else, then learn to use them.

Gazing down at my own body, I realized I was as misty as Iaga. I wasn't just lucid dreaming with the retired goddess - I was doing my version of dream walking.

What had pulled me out of my body and into the jungle, if not Iaga? I focused my mind back on the camp, the softness of the blanket, and the hard fae body that had been curled up behind me when I'd fallen asleep.

I felt myself floating back there, but I just wasn't quick enough.

CHAPTER EIGHT

CARLYLE

A new form slipped onto the jungle path, as silent as the moon that had broken through a gap in the canopy above. A black jaguar stood before my half-formed body, as high as my waist. He was so close I could see the soft gray hairs mixed into his muzzle and count the scars crossing his face.

His eyes were sharp and golden, though, and his tail flicked lazily in the night air.

I froze, hoping maybe he couldn't see me, since even Jai had been unaware of me the first time I'd done it.

That hope died fast when I felt the presence of three other jaguars closing in behind me. They were just as silent, but easy enough to sense with all the combinations of magic at my disposal. I smelled their faint furry tang, and through the dull ache where my fang-like horn would be, I felt the faint coursing of blood through their veins and hearts.

Something told me the gray-furred one was important, and I kept my attention on him, while also summoning a better lock on the camp where my body was. If this grew dangerous, could I just siphon my soul, or whatever piece of me was here in the jungle?

Could I siphon my body *here*?

Before I decided which to try, the jaguar rose onto two legs and shifted fluidly before my eyes. His torso was bare, but a sort of dark leather kilt covered him from waist to knees. His skin was a deep bronze, and he had a short beard shot through with gray. His eyes were large and the same brilliant gold as his jaguar from. The color was a little more yellow than Killian's, but the gaze was every bit as challenging.

"Why have you come into our home without permission?" he demanded. "It is trespassing, and there are consequences."

"Something drew me here - this magic only manifests when there's a strong need," I said, keeping my voice even and steering away from the fact that I didn't really know how to control this mind-body disconnection. "So, perhaps you should check your people."

Actually, I hadn't thought of my magic that way until the words came out, but Iaga's advice to trust myself still echoed in my ears. I'd done this for Jack and Jai when their desperation drew me near - someone was in trouble here.

The jaguars behind me growled, and the man before me narrowed his eyes.

"My *people* are none of your concern, and I would never trust a dreamwalker. Leave our jungle!"

"I'm not a dreamwalker, no matter how it looks. I came here to source a moonstone - maybe even a sunrise moonstone," I confessed, hoping to distract him from his antagonism.

"No," he said, crossing his arms over his broad chest.

One of the jaguars had circled around to my left side, and his fangs were practically grazing my non-body. I bit down on a few choice words.

"Look. I don't mean to pull the celebrity card here, but I'm the Qilin Queen who opened the Path again. Iaga blessed me with many powers, and appearing in this soul form without my body seems to be one of them. But I'm not perfect - I need a moonstone to heal some, ah, some things. And I need to do it fast, because Haret has a lot going on." I almost added a *please*, but the guy's face had pulled into a freaking annoying sneer as I talked.

"Then you're the one responsible for the chaos beyond the jungle. That makes me even happier to tell you no."

"Are you fucking kidding me?" I cried, the words tumbling out before I could stop them. "I'm not *responsible*. I'm trying to stop that shit. Now, how much for a moonstone?"

Another jaguar had pulled up on my right side, and I was getting pretty antsy, even in my misty state.

"No," he repeated, his voice lowering into a growl. "Sunrise moonstones are never bought - they can only be won by great sacrifice. And killing off darkbloods isn't the sort of sacrifice I'm talking about. Leave!" he snarled.

Fucking hell. I backed up a few steps, deciding this wasn't going anywhere good. I didn't have much access to my magic here, and the word *sacrifice* was making me all kinds of edgy. No matter what this guy thought I 'd done or was going to do, I was determined that no one else would die on my quest for these stones.

I closed my eyes, focusing hard on the camp where my body was - I needed to get back there and talk to my guys and Lata before doing anything else. Whatever customs and laws the jaguars observed, I'd obviously pissed them off with my accidental nighttime visit. And my earlier ah, war cry.

"Wait! She carries the lion's magic we've been waiting for," a female voice hissed, breaking my concentration.

My eyes flew open, and I whirled just in time to see a dark-haired woman toss a sort of filmy spiderweb net over my form. It stuck to the edges of my mind, and I felt like an insect whose wings have been pinned to a board. An odd, paralyzing tingle spread over me, and my weightless form suddenly seemed immovable.

Ah, *crap*. This was bad. I didn't even know enough about this magic to force myself back to my body, and now she'd somehow trapped me. But freaking why?

I wasn't even sure I could reach my guys' minds at this point - my magic and focus were both so scattered.

"What are you doing?" I demanded. "You wanted me to leave, but now you wrap me up like a bug?" I fought against the net, but the more I struggled, the more it stuck to me. I tried again and again to call out to Sol and Jack and Killian in my mind, but even that sounded faint.

The webbing constricted, pulling me to my knees on the jungle floor. Valda had warned me about the dangers of this bodiless state, and of course, she was always fucking right. I didn't have access to my full power like this. I was in some shit, for sure.

"We're taking that swirling orange magic, queenie," the woman said, laughing as she peered down at me. The gray-bearded man crowded in close, studying me.

"She claims to be a qilin, but I've never scented one," he said to the woman.

Now that I could see them both together, I

wondered if they were twins. She sneered at him and tucked back her gray-threaded hair.

"I have, and she's not lying. That's probably how she has the lion magic. I was right to call her here. Now back off and let me transfer it."

I fought even harder at that - what would happen if she took Sol's magic? I knew the mating bond would hold, but would it hurt us? And what did they even want with it? And how could she steal it?

My thoughts dissolved into a scream of pain and outrage as the woman pressed her fingers deep into my lower belly - practically *through* me, thanks to my flimsy form. The worst cramps I'd ever had wracked my body, and all I could do was curl around the pain.

Low growls and mewls from the other jaguars filled the air around me, and from the tiny slits of my eyes, I saw the jungle begin to glow with a soft orange light.

My soft orange light. *My* fucking lion magic.

But I was too weak to do anything about it. These assholes would have never had a chance if I'd waited and come to them in the morning, in my full form. Which left the question - had this woman really been the one to call me here, or was there an innocent stuck in the middle again?

"Now, for the curse!" the woman cried, cackling. "Set foot or spirit in this jungle again, and your precious lions will pay us in blood and land for generations!"

My body convulsed like I was dry heaving, but I

had no stomach in this form to actually expel anything. I'd heard of territorial creatures, but goddamn.

Her fingers drew away, the spiderweb magic clinging to them and sloughing from me like I was emerging from a cocoon.

"But we don't take without giving, do we, brother? For your trouble, Queen." The woman flourished both her hands, and for a hopeful second, I thought she might draw a moonstone from somewhere.

Ah, nope.

"Heed this well," the man said, leaning down into my face. "Tonight may look like a happy accident, but nothing is random in our encounter." He chuckled, and the sound crawled all over me.

Happy accident, my ass.

The woman leaned in, her cheek touching the man's, and my belly swam with nausea as I looked into the twin pairs of bright golden eyes.

The man chanted,

"Lion's roar and Mage's spells.
Watch Light turn to fire as we rebel.
More than one race will need a tomb:
A smothering curse around Haret swells."

I convulsed again, reeling with the horrible feeling of needing to vomit but having no stomach to do so.

The woman chanted,

"A rainbow blooms,
Heals a barren womb.
But a Queen tells secrets,
And Haret dooms."

The jaguars around me yowled and screamed in what sounded like triumph. The twins shifted into their huge cat forms, then bounded away with their entourage, my wispy orange lion magic trailing after them like smoke.

I was left staring up at the canopy, feeling weak enough that I worried I might have trouble finding my way back to my body. Minute by minute, I drifted a few inches toward camp.

Somehow, my form made it back to my mates, and as I opened my eyes in my real body, I found my three guys staring down at me in absolute panic.

"Thank fuck," Killian shouted, gathering me close to him. "Where did ya go, Savage?"

"None of us could reach you," Jack added, his fingers squeezing mine tightly. I saw Lata kneeling behind Sol, wide-eyed and open-mouthed.

"Sorry, guys," I rasped, but with the intake of humid, early-morning air, I felt the latent nausea slam into me full force.

Wrenching away from Killian, I vomited onto the ground, nothing but bile coming up. Sol scrambled to pull my hair from my face, and his presence brought to mind exactly what had just happened in the jungle. It had obviously not been any kind of dream.

Deep in my lower belly - right where the woman had dug her nails in - felt hollow and fragile. And I was so fucking weak.

Jack held a cup of water to my lips, and I swallowed down the cool liquid gratefully. "What the hell happened, baby?" he whispered, resting his forehead against my temple.

Sol took the cup from him and bent to look in my eyes. "Seriously, shortcake. What happened? I felt it through our mating bond - hell, all of us felt it."

I nodded, gathering my focus to tell the story. "I think the jaguars set it all up. Something pulled me into the forest, doing my dreamwalking thing. That's only ever happened when one of you was in trouble," I added, looking at Jack.

"But you didn't find anyone in trouble, did you?" Lata asked, and her flat tone of voice caught my attention.

"Did you know something?" I asked, peering at her in the growing light. Shit, I really had been out all night.

"Ah, not exactly. But I've heard the *jaguars* are in trouble. My source is a runaway. She told me these twin elders have basically taken over, and they're not very nice."

"Twins, huh. Yeah. Met them. Your source is good," I said, my eyes rolling back in my skull. Damn, I was exhausted.

"So, you're saying the jaguars themselves might have called Carlyle?" Sol asked, his head tilted in question at his sister.

She shrugged. "I have no idea how it works. But my source said the twins are planning something big, and that a lot of the jaguars want nothing to do with it."

"I think the woman called me, and I have no idea how, but she took my lion magic," I confessed, leaning back against Sol. My eyes felt so heavy - fatigue much deeper than simply missing a night of sleep was settling over me.

Sol growled, his muscles tensing beneath me. "So, that's what I felt. We're still mated, though. She just took the stores you had. You'll replenish soon," he promised.

I smiled weakly. I couldn't even summon the energy to get excited about that, which worried me as much as what the twins might want with my magic in the first place. I mean, I always wanted my mates.

"We have to get in there and get her magic back," Lata insisted. "It's more than getting it back for Carlyle more - those two shouldn't have it for whatever they're planning."

"And how do you expect us to find them?" Jack asked, his voice strained.

"She cursed me, too," I moaned, all of their fucking antics piling up on me like a crushing weight in my chest. "The woman said if I set foot in the jungle again, all the lions would pay in blood for generations."

Lata growled and shot to her feet, pacing like a

caged animal.

"Where does a jaguar get that sort of dark magic?" Killian asked, but nobody answered. It was highly unusual for shifters to have the capabilities these twins seemed to have.

"Probably working with a fae or a mage," Lata spit out. "Sorry," she added, looking at Kills. He shrugged and waved the comment away.

I opened my mouth to repeat the new riddle, too, but then something about its wording slammed into me. The Oracle's riddle had said something about a darkblood paying the price if I sang - and as soon as I'd shared the riddle, she'd been strung up from the rafters.

This riddle carried the same warning - *a Queen tells secrets, and Haret dooms.*

Fuck. Fuck, fuck, *fuck.*

I'd have to build a goddamn fortress around this intel in my mind, or Jai would ferret it out, even if I kept it from the guys here. I bit down on another curse, trying not to draw attention to myself.

"How the fuck are we supposed to get her magic back?" Sol growled, fixating on that piece of the nightmare. "It's too risky for her to go in the jungle."

Lata narrowed her eyes. "I think I have an idea. It would either scare them shitless or make them think they've won the jackpot. Either way, it gives us a shot." She looked at Killian. "Glamor me to look like Carlyle. I'll strut my ass back in there, and they'll either think they just won the pride, or they'll be terrified of Carlyle's power."

My men looked at each other, considering it. Really?

"Absolutely not," I cried, the effort bringing up another round of dry heaving. Wiping my mouth, I continued, "No fucking way are you risking yourself for me."

Lata gave me a determined look, but I shook my head.

"Sol," I pleaded. "What if she becomes a sacrifice?"

His face blanched as he connected my thoughts - I was terrified Lata would be the one who died this time.

"She's not a darkblood, though," Killian pointed out, and Jack nodded reluctantly.

"I'll be fine. Let's do it," Lata said, her mind obviously made up.

"I can manage-" I started, but Sol cut me off with a sweet kiss to my temple.

"I think it will work, shortcake. Let someone help you, for once."

My brow furrowed in worry, and I tried to think fast and come up with another plan. My mind was too tired, though, and I didn't see how I could stop them other than forbidding it.

I really didn't want to have that sort of relationship with my sweet lion.

"Just...just be safe," I whispered, hanging my helpless damn head.

"I'll stay with you," Jack said, reaching for me and settling me in his lap.

Killian nodded. "I'll go along to keep the glamor up - I'll need to stay close to really fool them. Fuckers might scent right through it. I promise, shortcake - one bad feeling and we're out of there." He gave Lata a stern look, and she rolled her eyes at him.

"Let's do this shit," Lata said, standing and facing the jungle. She tossed me a saucy look. "Goddess save the Queen, right?"

CHAPTER NINE

KILLIAN

I'd put up a good front for my Savage, but Sol and I exchanged a look as we left camp that told me he wasn't any too keen on the current plan, either.

Only Lata was excited, trotting ahead like a goddamn puppy out for a stroll. For now, I was keeping us all invisible and practicing using my air magic to blow away any hint of lion or fae.

I knew I could match Carlyle's visuals with my glamor - it was the scent I was worried about. It would take some serious fucking concentration to use both my glamor and my air magic to keep her smelling like Carlyle in the close jungle heat, and not a wet kitty. If the jaguars started to surround us, the air would have nowhere to go.

Our girl had looked miserable, though. In my mind, there was really no choice. This whole trip to the jungle had been Lata's idea, anyways, so it was admirable that she was taking responsibility for the shit we were in.

I'd hoped that would make me feel better about what the risks we were taking, but I still felt like an asshole for taking advantage of Sol's kid sister like this.

"If shit gets bad in here, get her out first," Sol told me, his voice a low growl. I nodded - it was a given.

The jungle loomed dark ahead of us, even though it was now broad daylight. I wished we knew more about these rogue jaguars - just what kind of magic did they have access to? Unfortunately, Lata's source had been a bit vague on that.

As we got closer, I stopped glamoring us invisible and began to weave the disguise around Lata, hearing Sol curse under his breath.

"That's fucking weird," he muttered, and I chuckled.

"Jus' keep reminding your dick that's your sister, lion," I warned. He gave me a dark look, and if we weren't about to enter enemy territory, I would have paid for my comment with a tussle.

I didn't bother to glamor myself since the twins had scented me out before anyway. I needed to keep all my power focused on maintaining Lata's cover.

Lata reached the very edge of the rain forest, turning back to look at us. "This *has* to stay civil," she reminded us. "I doubt you can glamor me up any of her magic."

That was the damn truth. We needed to be actors today, not fighters.

I saw Lata take a deep breath and square her shoulders. A fuck-all attitude I couldn't fake with glamor spread across her face, and I wondered how much she'd studied Carlyle to make the change so convincing.

She sauntered into the wild growth of the jungle, and Sol and I hurried to flank her as best we could along the narrow path.

"How do ya plan to find them?" I asked, scanning the area.

"Oh, they're here, all around us," Sol said under his breath. "Nobody sneaks into a big cat's territory."

I upped my air magic to take extra care with Lata's scent, directing any leftover lion smell toward Sol. He'd planned to stay right next to her just in case.

"I'm here to see the true leaders of this pack," Lata called into the dense growth. "Last night I was called here against my will and assaulted by unauthorized magic. As the Qilin Queen of Haret, I demand an explanation, or you'll have more trouble than you can handle."

I sensed a jaguar closing in on us from the left, but before I could motion to Sol, he was on it, shoving open the dense foliage to our left.

"Show yourself," he demanded, a deep, commanding growl rolling through his words. A small, sleek jaguar slunk onto the path just in front of where he'd looked, shifting in a smooth motion.

It was a female, probably close to Lata's age.

"Take us to the true leader," Lata repeated, but the girl shook her head, a look of worry crossing her face.

"He's not well. And we have no magic to assault you with."

Sol stepped slightly in front of Lata. "She was attacked by a small group, led by a male and female. Twins. They tried to curse the queen so she couldn't return here and retrieve the magic they stole without compromising my pride."

The girl hissed, shifting and darting deep into the jungle before any of us could react.

"Well, fuck." I frowned. "Did we jus' blow our chance?"

"I don't think so," Lata said, pursing her lips. "I'm guessing the coup my source was afraid of has progressed a bit, and we just stepped straight into the middle of it. I just hope that one's not on the twins' side."

"Fuckin' great," I grumbled. "Why can't we jus' get an easy break once in a while?"

SOL

I considered Lata's suspicions. She was probably right, and of course, this complicated things even more.

One way or another, the twins would find out we were here. But if the rightful leaders took advantage of our arrival to ask for help or back the twins into a corner, who knew what they'd do.

Wild animals of any race didn't react well to feeling trapped.

"Get on my back. We may need all the queenly sway you can muster up," I told Lata, kneeling to shift into my lion form. She mounted me, and I knew she'd keep her back straight and regal like a Queen was expected to look. Thanks to our mother's constant training, she definitely knew how to pull the right moves.

"Makes my job easier," Killian muttered, and I guessed he was still worried about keeping Lata's scent covered. The fae was better than he gave himself credit for, though - always had been.

I sensed the jaguars at almost the same time as Lata stiffened even more on my back. Breaking through an abnormally thick clump of brush, we came upon a network of rope bridges leading up to platforms and covered houses high in the trees.

The slim girl who had found us darted into sight ahead, shimmying up one of the rope ladders and into a central tree house.

I turned my lion's head toward Killian, tilting my

ears toward what I was seeing. After so many years together, we barely needed words. He nodded as he followed my attention - the leader's quarters were definitely up that tree.

But where were the twins?

Jaguars surrounded us on all sides, keeping their distance but causing a menacing effect in their number.

"I'm here to see the true leader," Lata called again, and a few low growls vibrated the air. My mane pricked along the back of my neck, and I felt Lata tensing on my back as she continued, "We don't mean any harm to your group. But harm was done to me last night, and I demand an explanation."

The girl reappeared in the doorway of the house we'd assumed were the leader's quarters. She called down to the crowd. "Escort the girl here - only her."

I didn't like that one fucking bit, but Lata pinched my ear as she slid off my back. I wasn't about to shift out of my more-intimidating form, as Killian was already getting some extra attention, too. It was probably rare to see a fae around here, and playing nice for politics was not one of his better qualities.

"I'll be fine," Lata whispered, her voice more fierce than frightened.

I was torn, but before I could make up my mind, three jaguars slid between Lata and us, and the rest formed a tight circle around Killian and me. Lata was guided to the rope ladder, and the three jaguars shifted to climb behind her.

Each of them were young males, well-muscled and quick on their feet.

My gut twisted in worry, but I forced myself to trust Lata's instincts. She hadn't gained the top spot in Mother's guard on family connections alone. That wasn't how the lions worked.

One of the jaguars near me shifted to his human form.

"Where did she see the twins? And when?" he demanded.

Killian stepped toward him, a little closer than he needed to be, and I grinned inside as the fae towered over the slim male. He crossed his bulky arms and glared before answering.

"None of us were with her, so I don' know. She can do somethin' like dreamwalk, and evidently those twins took advantage and called her here in her damn sleep. They attacked her - if it weren't for the Queen's strength, she might be in a lot of fuckin' pain."

I hoped the jaguars couldn't sense the worry I heard in our fae's voice. Carlyle *was* in a lot of pain. And her magical strength hadn't meant a goddamn thing in her dream form.

We should have had Valda spend some extra time with Carlyle after the coronation. The old vampire should have helped Carlyle learn a bit more - maybe then we wouldn't be in this mess.

"The twins have much to answer for," the male said, and I sensed a haunted double meaning to his words. Whoever these twins were to this community, they'd evidently hurt more than just our Qilin.

Just then, a shout from above called my attention to Lata. She was standing in a patch of sun just outside the leader's hut. I growled at Killian because it looked like her glamor was slipping.

"Na' me," the fae growled under his breath.

A bent form hobbled out of the hut and around Lata, coming to grasp the railing. The man looked ancient - his skin was leathery and sagged off his skull, and his back was as curved as the moons of Haret. I caught the flash of several large sunrise moonstones hanging from a leather cord around his neck, and my heart leaped, only to fall as I watched them.

The closer he got to Lata, the more her glamor faded.

The jaguars around us had grown silent, and I noticed they had all either kneeled or sat back on their haunches, listening with high respect.

Killian bowed his head, and I followed, hoping our luck was turning a bit.

"Who among you has information on the activities of Ezra and Evelyn?" the man called down, his voice warbling like a bird.

A young male stepped forward. "I saw them entering camp late last night, well after third rounds and the closing of the gates. They were sneaking in through the western entrance."

He pointed at what looked to me like just another clump of foliage. I'd seen no gates at all - did they have access to some sort of magical barrier?

The mix of magic here was just too odd for a shifter community.

And then I wondered why he hadn't reported the twins when he'd seen them. Was he working with them, and trying to save face now? Or had the fear of retaliation been too great until now?

"It is shameful for me to have lost control of my fosters," the man said, turning to Lata. I wasn't sure if Kills could hear his words, but my lion's ears were doing just fine picking up the conversation.

"I hold no grudge against your people. I just want what was stolen from me," Lata replied, keeping up the charade.

The man regarded her for a long moment. "Yet it is also shameful for you to attempt to deceive me. Why do you ask for help if you do not trust us?"

Lata's face colored, and she looked down at Killian. "Drop the glamor, fae."

Kills looked at me. I wasn't sure it was the best move, but I'd resolved to trust Lata. From our distance, we didn't have a great read on the man. I nodded, and Killian pulled in his magic, peeling away the image of Carlyle from my sister's form.

"I am sorry," she said, her voice harder to hear once the jaguars began gossiping. "The truth is that the twins' magic has hurt our Queen. I devised this plan to try and save face, but I think it was the wrong call. Can you please help us?"

"Your candor is appreciated," the leader replied. "We are proud as well, and it is not easy for me to admit my fosters have turned against us and against you in such a way."

"What do you mean, your fosters?" Lata asked. I'd been wondering it, too, but I wished she'd stay on topic.

"My own children died young, and I took Ezra and Evelyn in as my own when their family also perished. However, as they came of age, they resented my refusal to give control to them automatically. Some have chosen to follow them as they attempt to force my hand. And as you have unfortunately seen, I'm losing the battle."

Something in my heart was aching for this leader, and I knew Carlyle would want to help - would want us to help. I shifted, startling the nearby jaguars.

"Sir, please accept our apologies again. I'm Sol, son of Reina Jazira of the nearby lion pride. I'm also mated to the Queen, and I know she would love to aid you in any way possible as soon as her strength is restored. Any information you could give us about the twins' location or plans could help. We promise no harm to them," I added, going on instinct that maybe they'd gotten such free reign due to their adopted father's love and resulting lenience.

The old man nodded and turned to one of the males close behind him. They spoke low enough that I couldn't hear them, but after a few minutes, the leader beckoned to Killian and me.

"Please, join me in my home. We will discuss this further."

Lata caught my eye and nodded, giving her assessment of the situation.

"Are you good with this, fae?" I asked under my breath.

"Let's do it," Killian agreed, and the two of us headed up the rope ladder.

CHAPTER TEN

CARLYLE

I'd lost count of how many times I'd rolled to my side, dry heaving. There wasn't an ounce of liquid left in my body, and I was so pissed at that jaguar woman for whatever magic she'd used to fuck up my stomach.

Damn, my muscles ached.

Jack had been calm and reassuring, keeping my hair tucked back in a braid and a cool cloth on my forehead, but I could sense how worried he was.

And he didn't know the half of it.

I felt nearly as weak as I used to before I'd met the guys - like my lion strength was really *gone*. Not only that, but the magic I still felt was muddled, like it was mixed up even more than before.

I was hoping it was just my imagination, but all I could visualize when I looked inside for my beautiful rainbow was a murky mess.

Like what happens when you paint with too many watery colors, and they all just run together to make brown.

I was more grateful than ever that Jai wasn't with me because he would surely sense my thoughts. Then he'd probably shred every leaf in the jungle looking for the twins - which would spread even more rumors about a Queen who hated darkbloods.

I groaned, rolling onto my back and staring up at the blue sky. It was hot, too.

"Want some water?" Jack asked, holding a cup up so I could see it.

"I want to sink straight down into it," I grumbled. The morning was growing warmer every minute, and sweat was trickling down my temples and collarbone. I raised up a little, letting him tip some of the cold water into my mouth.

Hopefully, this time it would fucking stay down.

I'd tried a few times to reach Sol or Kills through our mental connection, but even that was too taxing for me right now. I hated feeling this useless, but of course, there was nothing I could do about it.

"They'll be back soon with that moonstone, and we'll get all your power sorted where it should be," Jack said, and I didn't call him out on having said it at least twice before. "Wait - what's that?" he asked, shooting to his feet.

I struggled to a sitting position and scanned the jungle's edge where he was pointing.

"That's them!" I cried, recognizing the female twin's long, gray-streaked hair even from this distance. I barely had time to warn Jack to be careful before he'd shifted and taken to the air.

I'd never make it there if he needed me, but I hauled myself to standing anyway.

The male whirled and drew a bow, loosing an arrow straight up at my dragon. Jack roared and swerved, but a second arrow ripped into his left wing. I stumbled back to my knees as I felt the twinge of pain through our mating bond, but Jack didn't falter.

He dodged a third arrow, but then the female launched a spear, and Jack took another, bigger hit to his wing.

A hoarse scream rattled out of my throat, and the male turned in my direction. I was too far away to make out his expression, but he bolted toward me. I scrambled back to my feet, swaying from dehydration.

Jack flapped crookedly between us, though, slamming into the ground, nearly on top of the male jaguar.

I heard a scream of pain, and Jack snapped at something on the ground. I grimaced - *please don't eat him,* I begged Jack in my mind, but I didn't think my magic was strong enough for him to hear me.

Jack rolled up to his scaly feet, though, and I saw

the male crouch and shift. He bounded out of Jack's reach, but I could see one of his legs was hanging at an awkward angle. The female had shifted back to her jaguar form too, and they streaked along the jungle edge.

Before Jack could lumber after them or take to the sky, they suddenly vanished, like they'd fallen down a cliff.

Ah, if only it were that easy.

Jack circled back toward me, shifting as he hit the ground and tumbling toward me.

"Are you okay, honey?" he asked, kneeling to check me out.

"Of course. You're bleeding, though," I pointed out, checking where the weapons had left marks on his arm and ribs. "Where the fuck did they go?"

"Some kind of trap door hidden in the grass. Underground tunnel, maybe? I'd really like to check it out more, though," he said, giving me the side eye.

"Don't worry about me, dragon. I'm too weak to fucking walk over there, but I can park my happy ass near the fire for a few more minutes. I've got my knives and enough magic to torch someone."

I fucking hated trying to convince Jack I wasn't in trouble, but it was true. My magic was there, but it was as weak as my muscles. But I wanted him to go after those goddamn twins. I just had to make sure he felt safe enough leaving me.

"Hopefully, the others will have better luck than us," I grumbled, clenching my stomach muscles against another wave of nausea. I tried to distract myself by digging in Sol's pack for something to clean and bandage Jack.

JACK

As soon as my girl would let me go, I took to the air again. I hadn't wanted to leave her, but if I could catch those fucking jaguars, we could get Carlyle what she needed. Circling above, I followed the line of the jungle over and over again, trying to pinpoint where they'd disappeared. At first glance, I'd thought they'd fallen off something in their haste, but the ground was flat and final.

It had to be an escape route. That had even more bad implications - it meant they'd been planning some serious shit.

There - I caught a glimpse of a dip in the ground beneath the waving meadow grass that bordered the jungle. Flying lower, I decided to fuck it all and let loose a thick stream of fire. The grass shriveled and burned in seconds.

Beneath, it looked like the tunnels left by some kind of burrowing animal, like a fucking gopher. Only bigger, of course.

But as far as an entrance was concerned, I had nothing. Not a single visual.

Cursing, I flew lower and lower until my claws

nearly dragged the ground. I needed to find something - fuck, I needed to come back to my girl with *something*.

Then a spark of magic coursed through my claw, rippling up my leg. It reminded me of the sort of barrier Dair always put up for our safe houses. Trying to land sent a jolt of electricity through me, and I shot back into the air, worried about what effect that might have on Carlyle.

I had to stop my hunting now before it made things worse.

She'd hidden her pain well, but I knew the wounds in my wing and side had gotten to her through our mating bond.

Fuck, I needed the mage for this one. Or at least the vampire and his alien hearing.

Whirling back to camp, I found Carlyle flat on her back, breathing hard.

"Fuck, dragon," she managed as I shifted and gathered her to me. "What the hell did you get into out there?"

"Sorry, honey," I answered, feeling like shit. "I found a tunnel, but it's spelled. We need Dair."

"Too bad he's playing puppet in Patriam again," she grumbled. "Don't worry, Jack. We'll make do. The others will be back soon."

I hated that she was basically repeating herself, trying to make me feel better when she was the one in fucking trouble.

"Do you think the jaguars are remembering old

magic, like the dragons and Qilin have been?" she asked after a few moments of silence.

I shrugged, stretching the stiffness from my muscles. "I've never heard of cat shifters who could summon you in a dream or put up a magical barrier. But I guess it's possible."

"Anything's possible," she murmured, leaning back into me.

I wished I had more answers for her - that any of us had more answers. But at least we were on our way to finding them, however convoluted the path might get.

"Rest, honey," I said, holding her tighter in my arms. "I'll keep watch. Get your strength back."

KILLIAN

Sol and I were sitting on either side of Lata, listening patiently to the old jaguar leader tell us a pretty shitty story of how his foster children were staging the coup we'd heard about. It was the kind of story that would activate Carlyle's savior issues for sure.

But I couldn't help but notice that I was paying the most attention, for once. One of the male jaguars had shifted into a bare-chested young man, and his gaze was resting on Lata often enough for her to notice and start to gaze a little back.

Not to mention Sol - the fucker's big-brother

instincts had activated and were nearly overruling the reason we'd come here in the first place.

"I'm certain our Qilin Queen would love to help you with this problem, but we really need to figure a way to heal her first," I said quickly, taking advantage of the old man stopping to catch his breath. I turned and glared at Sol.

He snapped out of his moodiness and nodded. "We initially hoped to gain a sunrise moonstone to heal her, um, earlier illness."

Lata bristled at the word, but we didn't have time for drama. Of course, problems getting pregnant weren't a damn illness, but we also had no business sharing Carlyle's business. I cut her off before she could correct Sol. "Perhaps one of those stones you have would make a nice gift for the Queen. Not sayin' she wouldn't help you otherwise, but she also can't go around solving every little problem in Haret."

"Isn't that what a Queen should do?" one of the females asked, narrowing her eyes.

"Carlyle loves helping others - it's the only reason the Path is even open," Lata snapped. "But that doesn't mean everyone wants her meddling. Haret needs help, sure. But she can't afford any more rumors about darkbloods."

The elder nodded. "I have heard these stories. This is possibly one reason Ezra and Evelyn targeted her."

"To provoke?" Sol asked. "Or in retaliation for some imagined attack?"

The leader only shook his head as though he had no idea why his kids might have dragged Carlyle into this shit. Honestly, the whole thing sounded off to me - I'd always thought of jaguar shifters as fierce. This group was no more than a bunch of black kitties hiding under the jungle canopy.

I was tapping my fucking toes when the leader finally nodded. He lifted his necklace of moonstones off his neck and spread it on the floor before him. I had to stop myself from snatching it up - we really needed to get back to our girl.

"You may take this one, but beware the power it holds. It pushes back darkness, of course, but it also contains enough warmth to attract the very, very cold in our world." He worked the binding off of the largest stone and handed it to Lata.

She grinned so hard even I couldn't help but smile - the kid was so proud of completing her plan to help us. The stone was nearly the size of her palm, too, smooth and creamy orange streaked with pale iridescence. It really looked like a sunrise moon, and although I'd grown up with fae magic, I was drawn to it.

No fucking idea how this rock would help Carlyle get better, but finally having it in hand was making my adrenaline pump - time to get the hell out of this jungle and check on Carlyle.

"Thank you," Sol said, bowing low as he got up. He was antsy, too. "We will return to help your people, I promise."

The elder gave us a cool look that said he didn't particularly believe Sol's words, but Lata repeated the promise several times as she backed out of the hut. Honestly, I didn't care much about their problems - we couldn't save every fucking family in Haret by ourselves.

We scrambled down the rope ladder and booked it out of the jungle. Of course, I sensed the jaguar escorts behind us, but I didn't even bother to turn and acknowledge them.

Sol shifted and bounded ahead with the stone in his mouth, but Lata trailed a bit, glancing over her shoulder for the jaguars following us.

"You can come back and flirt later, cub," I called back, and her anger flared at me. I just shrugged, though, as she sped past me. Objective accomplished.

"Fuck off," she hissed just before shifting and shooting into the growth. Grinning at how obvious she was being, I added what I could to my speed. I may not have lion legs, but I knew the way back.

By the time I cleared the jungle and could see Carlyle, Sol had already started trying to treat her with the stone.

Her shirt was pulled up to expose her belly, and the stone was resting on her lower stomach, a couple of inches below her navel.

"Sure that's the right *sruth*?" I asked. The rock was damn near resting on top of her pussy. I was sort of teasing Sol, but I wasn't completely certain, either.

"Jai's intel," he replied, his voice gruff with worry.

We were all crowded around Carlyle, and I could tell she was feeling it. Glaring up at us all, she made a shooing motion. "Let Sol concentrate. I'm not dying, but I might vomit on your shoes," she warned.

Lata and Jack backed up, but I didn't budge. Lata had started up her stupid pacing again when Jack sighed.

"Lata - maybe can you help me check something out?" he asked, watching Carlyle with a worried expression. "Maybe you too, Kills."

"Of course," Lata said, looking eager to help again. I rolled my eyes at him but followed his lead when Sol waved us away, too.

As Jack led us back along the jungle's perimeter, I noticed he had a bit of blood on his shirt above his ribs. He just shook his head when I raised my eyebrow at him.

He pointed at the grassy clearing before us. "We saw those fucking twins out here while you guys were gone. They disappeared down some sort of tunnel or some shit."

Lata growled and scanned the horizon where Jack was pointing. It didn't take us long to reach the spot, but finding the tunnel was another story.

"It was like they jumped in a goddamn rabbit hole." Jack was shaking his head as he edged around the burned section. Each of us had already gotten a good fucking shock when we'd strayed too close. I agreed - it was just like the barriers Dair made.

We hadn't found any sign of the entrance, either,

and it was pissing me the fuck off.

"These twins are fucking trouble," Lata grumbled, as if we didn't all know it. "I just hope they don't come anywhere near my lions."

"You need to get your ass back home then, and soon," I warned. "We're coming up with nothing here, and they had a hell of a head start."

Her brow furrowed in real worry, and she glanced back to where Sol and Carlyle were.

"Yeah, I still don't see a damn thing here," Jack affirmed, throwing his hands up. "Go on and check with Sol. Take care of your family, Lata."

Her jaw tensed, but she nodded before speeding away.

"I don't like this one fucking bit," Jack said in a low voice. "I don't know of any shifters who can do what those jaguars did. And to disappear like that…"

"Fuckin' mage work," I grumbled, and he nodded in agreement. "Maybe potions?"

Jack shrugged. "We need to get back and have a chat with Dair if he's done with those assholes in Patriam. For now, though, we just need to concentrate on getting our girl home. Jai's gonna fucking bust a blood vein."

I groaned, realizing he was goddamn right.

"Maybe you should just fly her home, and we'll follow," I suggested.

Jack snickered. "You think that will save you from the boss? Not fucking likely."

We did one final scour of the area before

admitting we had nothing, then jogged back toward Sol and Carlyle. Our Qilin was looking paler than usual, but at least she wasn't retching anymore.

CHAPTER ELEVEN

CARLYLE

"I really don't think I can fly," I said, grimacing at Killian and Jack's suggestion that Jack speed me home on his back. My stomach was rolling at the thought of it, and I was still sprawled in the grass.

"It's okay, shortcake. We'll take it home as slowly as you need," Sol reassured me, his hand warm on my belly, holding the sunrise moonstone in place. They all still looked super worried, though, and I was too. I'd never had a weak stomach, and I could only remember a handful of times I'd ever even been sick enough to vomit.

Nothing at all like this.

Sol turned to Lata, his expression already apologetic. "I know I should go home with you and help you tell all this crap to Mother, but I-"

"No worries," Lata interrupted, her tone a little too flippant.

"We can come-" I started, but Sol shut me up with the bossy sort of look Jai was usually best at. For some reason, seeing it on my lion's face stirred something deep in my belly - something that definitely wasn't nausea. His eyes widened and flashed at me.

Without looking up at his sister, he said, "Head home now, Lata. Tell Mother to come to the castle if she really wants to chew my ass. I need to take care of *this* one."

The heat in my core flared even higher with those cryptic words, and I sensed Jack and Killian had perked up and were paying closer attention.

"Thanks a lot, big brother," Lata grumbled, but a small smile hovered at the edge of her mouth. I could tell that even though she wasn't looking forward to her mother's anger, she was totally okay with stepping away from our mounting tension. After all, she'd already gotten quite the show.

"Thank you, Lata. Seriously. I think this stone is really going to help. I owe you big time," I promised, and she flushed. I wasn't lying, either. Even though we'd only been trying the stone for a few minutes, I was feeling a bit stronger. Like at least I could make it home.

"The jaguars will be a powerful ally for the lions, if Mother plays this well," Sol reminded her.

"We *will* play it well," Lata agreed, and I grinned at her confidence. Reina Jazira had been running a tight ship all her life, but Lata was prepared to take the helm at any point, no matter what. She leaned in to hug Sol, waved to the rest of us, and shifted into her sleek lioness form.

"I like her," I murmured, watching her bound away until she was out of sight.

When I looked up at my men, though, it was obvious they were no longer thinking of Sol's kid sister.

"How do ya feel, Savage?" Killian asked, his voice pitched low.

Scanning each of their faces, I realized I was actually feeling a little like prey. It wasn't a new sensation, but I wasn't quite ready to test if my stomach could handle physical exertion. It might be fun to toy with them a bit instead.

"Good enough to ride," I said, lifting an eyebrow, and Killian smirked, crowding in closer. "But just my lion - no dragon yet."

A shadow of disappointment flashed over Killian's face as he realized I wanted to ride Sol's back, not his cock. But the idea was out there, and the heat between the four of us simmered.

It was weird to realize that for once, I *wasn't* feeling up for sex. My whole body was fucking weak, and worry about my magic coursed through me. It wasn't what I wanted, either, but maybe when it was time for a pit stop, I'd be ready for my men.

Sol shifted without a word, lowering to his belly so I could easily climb on his back.

"Put this in your pants until you're ready for something bigger," Jack said, winking at me as he held out the stone.

I giggled and slid the moonstone beneath my waistband. It was an odd sensation for sure, but as we started the slow pace home, I began to tune into the faint pulse of energy in the stone.

And not just energy - magic.

Even though we were traveling under the heat of midday sun, something cool coursed through the stone, like the white moonlight it was partially named for.

I closed my eyes and allowed Sol and the others to take care of logistics. I focused my attention completely on the smooth stone pressed against my skin, and the growing sense that something deep inside me really was responding. Just like sunrise promises a new day, I was feeling hope rise in my mind.

Suddenly, I was anxious to get home. I was eager to try all the stones I'd collected together. We hadn't tried placing any of them against my skin - against my *sruth*. Now, I was wondering why the hell not. I shouldn't have to collect all the stones to begin the healing.

After all, I'd gained all my colorful powers one at a

time.

Plus, I needed to get home and relieve some of the guilt I was feeling about not telling Jai the altered plan. Lata and I had more in common on that front than I'd care to admit. I snickered to myself at the idea of comparing Jai to Reina Jazira, but I couldn't help it.

They were both overprotective and overbearing, but for all the right reasons.

Eventually, though, the gentle rhythm of Sol's padding steps and the sway of his spine beneath me tempted me to lean into his mane, breathing deeply of the summer sun scent he always carried.

Before I knew it, Jack was shaking me awake, and the sun had set.

"We're stopping for the night, honey. Almost halfway home," he whispered, helping me slide off my lion. Sol stretched and flicked his tail, his wide mouth opening in a toothy yawn.

"Sorry - are you worn out?" I asked, rubbing the sleep from my eyes.

He gave a growly sort of laugh and shifted back. "Not hardly, shortcake. I'm hungry, though. How's your stomach?"

I made a face. "Food does *not* sound good. But at least I don't feel like vomiting." I spotted a large, sprawling tree ahead, and I headed for it on stiff legs. It would make good cover for the night. "I'm thirsty, though," I added.

"I'll go down there and see if there's water,"

Killian offered, pointing to a grove of the same trees, farther to the left of the path.

"Thank you," I called, the words barely making it out of my mouth before I was sinking against the tree's massive trunk. Damn, I was weak.

Jack was beside me in a second, his palm on my forehead, and his arm cradling under my shoulders.

Sol kneeled next to me, too, tipping what was left of his water past my lips.

"I fucking hate feeling like this," I muttered, my eyes sliding closed. "It's like the bitch took my strength *and* my healing."

I heard a snicker, and slitted open one eye. Jack was grinning.

"Got your strength and healing right here, honey," he said, gesturing to himself and Sol.

My other eye popped open. "You're not wrong, dragon," I answered, suddenly wondering why that sort of solution hadn't occurred to me before.

"Probably because you were too busy retching into the grass," Sol answered, proving that even now, I was still saying shit out loud that I'd meant to think.

But they were both eying me like they were totally up for some sexy fun, just too worried to ask for it. And maybe a bit of battery charge was just what I needed to shake this fatigue.

"Well, I don't have the energy to play back, but this is me giving consent, boys. Have your ways with me," I said, lifting my arms like a kid waiting to be stripped for bath time. "I mean it," I said, grinning at

Sol - I could tell he was already second-guessing the idea.

Jack just chuckled and tugged my shirt up over my breasts. "As you wish," he whispered, leaning in to suck one of my nipples, while his fingers teased and pinched the other.

"Shouldn't be too hard to give you a little shot of magic without you helping," Sol agreed, half teasing and half justifying.

I winked at him and leaned my head back against the tree, thoroughly enjoying my dragon's oral skills. Sol peeled my pants down, leaving the stone resting just below my navel. Within seconds, he'd launched quite the challenge to Jack by licking a solid line through my folds and swirling around my clit.

Sighing with bliss, I went limp and let them position me however they wanted. Soon enough, Jack had slid beneath me, cushioning my body from the hard ground. Sol hovered above us, kneading my thighs and dropping teasing kisses right where I wanted them.

Jack cradled my chin and twisted my neck until I could kiss him, and I felt Sol spreading my wetness lower. His fingers eased inside my ass, and I realized what they were planning.

"Okay?" Sol growled.

"I totally approve," I managed, as Sol's fingers stretched and readied me. He pressed my thighs wider and lifted my hips just enough for Jack to position himself. My dragon eased his hard cock into my ass so carefully I almost snapped at them.

I wasn't going to break, damn it.

But then Jack began to move, and Sol joined the fun in the front, pushing deep in my pussy with a groan that sounded suspiciously like a prayer. I was pinned between them, pliant and feeling pampered as hell.

My two sweetest mates held me as carefully as a rose, and soon my body was flushing and blossoming just for them.

"Goddamn, I miss all the fun," a surly, teasing voice called.

"Who said so?" I managed, lifting up to nip at Sol's lip. "I bet there's some fine lion ass in the air right now."

I felt Sol's breath hitch against my chest, and it was like my power to sense his emotions suddenly turned back on. I felt anticipation and excitement crackle across his skin as Killian stepped closer.

Sol turned his head and looked up at the fae, his golden blond curls glinting in the rising moonlight. Whatever silent words passed between them were enough. Killian yanked open his buckle and shimmied out of his pants so fast I almost giggled and ruined the hot moment.

I felt Jack tense a bit beneath me as Kills loomed above us, naked and glorious. My dragon was open-minded but had proved to be a little on the shy side. I leaned my head back into the crook of his neck, running my tongue along his jaw and ear. He moaned softly and turned his mouth to mine, welcoming the distraction.

I poured what little energy I had into the kiss, even as I thrilled at the added weight of Killian easing his cock into Sol. For a second, I worried Jack might feel squashed by all of us.

My lion's massive arms braced on either side of us though, his gorgeous muscles bunching up and holding himself off my chest just enough that Killian's fucking wouldn't completely take over the slow pace they had started.

I felt the change in mood and rhythm immediately anyway - Killian was never as careful as Sol or Jack, and I reveled in the delicious contrast swirling around me.

Sol struggled to maintain control as Kills drove him fast and hard to the edge, and even Jack seemed to be barely resisting the heady draw. I lifted my legs, wrapping my ankles around my lion and fae as much as possible, and ran my fingernails up and down Jack's sides.

My body was waking up in the most delicious ways again.

Each of their magics began to flow into me, bolstering me and reminding me of just what those fucking twins had taken.

Rage began to bubble just beneath the surface of my lust, and I felt energy spark back to life, beginning in my core. The moonstone on my belly seemed to blister with heat, and I felt Sol wince as he was driven harshly against me.

Killian shouted his release first, and I grinned and claimed Sol's lips, reveling in his quickened breath. I fucking loved it when my fae let loose like this. Jack moaned as he felt Sol's answering shudder rattle through my body, and soon my dragon was coming, too.

Killian shoved Sol to the side, and my lion huffed out a surprised laugh as the fae dropped to his knees before me.

I wasn't laughing, though, because Killian had buried his mouth in my pussy, sucking at every swollen part of me and lashing deep with his tongue. I realized he was tasting Sol and me together, and this thought tumbled me right over the edge.

I cried out as my body shook and my core pulsed with pleasure. My eyes rolled back in my head as I was passed from one set of strong arms to another. I felt someone wipe me gently with a cool cloth, and a blanket settled over my chest and shoulders.

Grinning like the satisfied Qilin I was, I blinked up at the stars just waking above me. My men had given me a hell of a shot of strength and healing, but I'd been so depleted that right now I was ready for a full night's sleep.

"Goddamn, boys. That one's a repeat," I said through a yawn. They were all looking pretty pleased with themselves as they finished setting up a basic camp and snuggled me between them all.

"As you wish," Jack whispered again, his grin sly as

he set himself up for first watch.

Sol wrapped his arm around my waist, keeping the moonstone pressed to my skin, and Killian buried his nose in the crook of my neck. I drifted to sleep dreaming of swirls of orange magic emanating from the stone, and something in me settled, knowing that I was on the right path.

I might not know exactly what the next step was, but I was ready for it.

CHAPTER TWELVE

CARLYLE

I opened my eyes to a gorgeous sunrise, but as soon as I started to stretch, my stomach flipped me the middle finger. I scrambled desperately away from Sol's arms and retched onto the nearby grass.

"Fucking hell," I managed, my voice raspy. My throat was raw from stomach acid - I didn't even have any food to throw up. My men were already crowding around me in worry, holding my hair and rubbing my back as my body tried like hell to expel a whole lot of nothing.

"Honey, you have to drink," Jack warned as I

rolled back onto the blanket, completely spent.

"It will just make me puke again," I complained. I knew he was right, though. I had to stay hydrated. Grumbling to myself, I accepted a water flask and took tiny sips while my guys started packing up camp.

Killian ripped open a parcel of Lata's dried meat, though, and one whiff of the smell sent me scurrying back to the grass.

Sol handed me a cloth to wipe my mouth.

"Sorry, it's just the smell. It's like I'm even more sensitive now," I said, reassuring Kills. His face was shadowed with guilt. "Go on. You guys have to eat, even if I can't."

"Take it over there," Sol suggested, so Kills and Jack walked a few dozen feet away to eat. I snuggled into Sol, wondering what the hell was wrong with my body, and when it was ever going to end.

Sol took a turn eating from a distance, and soon we were back on the road, me riding my lion again.

Thankfully, the journey home seemed to go quickly. I entertained myself by counting how long I could hold down sips of water, and as the day wore on, I was feeling much better. We entered the forest surrounding the castle just after sunset, and I was almost immediately greeted by a flash of vampire speeding through the trees.

"Tell me everything," Jai commanded, gathering me from Sol's back. "I lost all my connection with you, and I-"

"It's okay, boss," I reassured him, reeling from the

intensity of his worry that was seeping into me from his touch.

Sol gave Jai a quick version of the story, and I could feel Jai's muscles tighten like he was ready for another fight. Luckily, he didn't direct any of that anger at my lion - there was no way I had the strength to break up another scuffle between them.

Toro met us at the castle's kitchen door, which was where we often entered from the forest, through the gardens. It was usually a handy entrance to pick up a snack and a bit of gossip. But today…

"Oh shit," I muttered as I caught a whiff of shifter cakes baking. Jai wasn't quick enough to let me go, and I ended up spitting what little water I'd kept down onto his shoes.

"Get her out of the kitchen," Jack cried, exasperation making his voice sharper than usual. Jai sped me through the castle corridors and into our massive bedroom, where thankfully, there were no lingering food odors.

"This is a problem," my vampire said, glaring at his shoes.

"I'm assuming you're not talking about your boots," I answered with my own scowl. "And yeah, I know it's a problem. But what else is fucking new? The moonstone is helping, but we need more. More stones, more intel, more everything."

Exhaustion rippled through me, and I slumped against the pillows.

Nothing sounded good - not coffee, not sugar.

Nothing. This officially fucking sucked.

"We need those stones," I muttered again.

"I'll get the ones we have," Jai replied, speeding out of the room.

Toro eased onto the bed with me, combing my messy hair back with his fingers. "We'll figure out what's wrong with you, baby girl. We'll fix it."

I leaned into him, loving the mood but hating the idea that I was broken. I felt miserable, sure. But broken? My soul rejected that idea instantly.

"Dair?" I asked, missing my mage, but Toro shook his head.

"Not yet, but as soon as he's back, we'll ask him about any potions that might help, too."

Sol, Killian, and Jack had settled around me on the bed when Jai returned with the stones. He set about stripping my clothing gently. The moonstone stayed in its place on my lower belly. The leprechaun's heart stone went between my breasts, and the singing stone from the Oracle rested in the middle of my forehead.

I knew I needed to read up on my *sruth*, but luckily, my vampire had been studying.

"Rest, *aima*," Jai whispered, stretching out near my feet. "Let the stones' energies soak into you."

I gave him a thumbs-up, afraid nodding would make the singing stone slide off. Sleep sounded good.

SOL

Carlyle drifted into sleep much faster than I'd expected, given that she'd rested so much on the way home. It worried me.

"I don't like this," Jai growled, and the others all gave their grumbles and curses of agreement.

"How can some shifter magic even cause this? I feel like we gotta be missing something," Toro said, shaking his head. He looked at Jai, and something unspoken passed between them.

"What is it, boss?" Killian asked, noticing too. "Did ya find something in the grotto?"

Toro sighed, and we all sat up a little straighter. Carlyle slept on, still as Sleeping Beauty.

"We swam deep. There are a lot of trenches and tunnels - some look like they might not be natural. And there's a…a thing down there. Not exactly a sea witch. Maybe a cursed fae. I just don't know."

"Can it get inside?" Jack asked, his eyes darting to the doorway like it might be there right now.

Jai shook his head. "I don't think so. We sealed the cracks where it might have been able to before. But the magic is different than anything I've seen."

"Does anyone else find this whole shit storm just a little bit odd - we have jaguar shifters with unseen magic, and now some creature?" I asked, the hair on the back of my neck standing up. What the fuck was going on in Haret?

"There's more," Jai admitted, and the tone of his

voice nearly stopped my heart. It was about Carlyle. I knew it. "When we were in Paris, and when Toro was here with Carlyle, we each saw…something. Something instead of her."

A choked noise came from Killian, and I felt like my world was spinning.

"A dark form," I said, and the others looked at me with understanding dawning. All except Jack.

"What are you talking about?" he demanded, peering over at Carlyle's sleeping form.

I looked at Jai. "Lata saw it, too. On accident - Carlyle dropped the barrier in the middle of our fucking. But her skin was dark, and her eyes were pure light. Like a glamor."

Toro and Jai nodded, agreeing that they'd seen something similar. Kills cursed, and I knew by the way he was scrubbing his hand through his hair that he'd seen it, too.

"I don't think she knows it's happening," Jai said quietly. I frowned, turning the memory over in my head. Lata had assumed it was a joke or a trick. But looking at it this way, in this context, Carlyle hadn't seemed to know.

And she certainly wouldn't still be playing the same joke. Our girl could barely keep a straight face when she threw out puns - something this elaborate just wasn't her style. Not to mention the creepiness factor.

"So, are we sayin' that some *thing* in the grotto is leaching onto our girl?" Killian asked, his voice rising.

Jai hissed at him to be quiet. "We don't know anything for sure. But we need to watch her much more carefully. We need to analyze when it started, and who's seen it, and why."

"We need to draw it out," Jack suggested, and everyone turned to him. He shrugged. "I mean, I haven't seen this *dark form*. But it's only happened during sex, yeah? That should be easy enough to try."

"What about a mirror?" Toro said slowly. "If it happens and she sees it, too…"

"That might work," I agreed. We all looked at Jai.

He sighed, and I could tell he didn't love it. But after a few seconds of contemplation, he nodded. "Set it up. Mirrors. And restraints. Whatever is in the grotto is deadly."

A shiver raced up my spine. If our girl had some sort of…some sort of parasite… it would explain a few things. Not all, but a few.

It was only a matter of minutes before we'd dragged a mirror in from the bathroom. But the restraints were a little trickier.

"Too bad Dair's not here," Jack snickered. "But I found some rope." He held it up, grimacing at it.

"Are we sure she'll be up for this? Being sick and all?" Toro asked, glancing with concern at our girl. She was still out cold.

"We'll take it slow. She was up for it last night, with Jack and me. She just let us do the work," I added, grinning to myself.

"Ya mean she let *me* do the work," Kills corrected,

shoving at my shoulder. I tossed him a smirk - he hadn't exactly hated the evening.

"We'll minimize. Toro and I will watch," Jai decided.

"Aw, damn," Toro pouted, and I couldn't help but chuckle at him. Poor bastard.

Jai stayed just as serious faced as ever. "We were the ones who saw the creature - we need to be on the lookout for any sign, no matter how small. We can't be distracted."

"You're never distracted, boss," Toro scoffed, and the vampire flashed some fang at him.

"He is when he drinks," Jack teased.

"I don't drink," Jai hissed, but then understanding washed over his face. "Stop, both of you. We have no reason to waste time like this."

Jack caught my eye, chewing on his lower lip. I could tell he was on the verge of laughing, but we both swallowed it down. This was complicated enough without a pissed-off vampire in the mix.

"Am I really supposed to tie her up?" Killian complained, holding up the rope Jack had brought. "That's more the mage's style. I prefer to use my hands," he added with a smirk, flexing his fingers and popping a knuckle or two. That reminded me of how Carlyle had gone a little wild when I'd gripped her neck that night by the fire.

"Hands, yes. On her neck," I blurted, feeling my skin flush when Killian raised his eyebrows at me. He'd sometimes enjoyed a bit of light choking, too.

"This is getting too technical for me," Jack said, stepping back into the shadows of the bedroom corner where Jai and Toro had retreated. "Kills the mood, yeah?"

"Guess it's up to us, then, fae," I growled. "Wake her up."

"Maybe a bit of suck an' fuck? Except let's reverse. I want top," he whispered, and something deep in me thrilled at the change. I nodded, and we both crawled onto the bed. Killian undid his pants and shoved them off, and I did the same, trying not to think about having an audience.

I settled myself at Carlyle's bare toes, while Killian slipped an arm beneath her shoulders. He began to kiss and suck at her neck, his fingers toying with her nipples. Carlyle moaned in her sleep, her thighs pressing together. I reached for her feet, massaging her arches and tugging her legs apart a little at a time.

"What time is it?" she asked groggily, but nobody answered. Killian covered her lips with his, and she sighed into the kiss. I could feel her strength still lagging - her limbs were limp in my hands. Even if these stones *were* helping, it was going to be one hell of a slow recovery.

Kills slowly maneuvered her until her back rested on his stomach, and I'd taken advantage of the movement to spread her legs wide. Killian's thick cock rested on her inner thigh, and her delicate fingers were fondling his tip. He sat up straighter, propping her high enough that she could get a good look at me.

"This is a nice way to wake up," she said, smiling down at me. I only winked at her and kissed a light trail up her thigh. She wriggled at the ticklish touch, and Killian's cock bounced toward me.

He groaned as I caught it in my mouth, taking him deep. At the same time, he plunged his fingers into Carlyle's pussy, and she cried out. I felt his hips buck, sending him even deeper, and I clamped down on my gag reflex. The heat of my girl's stare was blistering - she was into it.

I didn't want Killian to jar her, though, so I raised up on my elbows, bobbing my head up and down on his cock. Carlyle's fingers wrapped tightly in my hair, and my cock jerked at the idea of her guiding me along his shaft. I could glimpse his fingers rubbing her clit, and her legs twisted around my back.

The stones had all fallen off, but the fact that she wasn't vomiting or resisting was promising.

"Enough," Killian rasped, reaching down to shove me away. I wiped the edge of my lip and grinned at the two of them. Killian rose onto his knees, his muscles bunching as he brought Carlyle with him. She was like the figurehead carved on a ship - a beautiful siren goddess.

Our cocks rubbed against each other as I closed in to kiss her, pinching at her nipples. Kills pumped my shaft with his fist a few times before bowing Carlyle enough to slip inside her.

She cried out as he stretched her, but it turned into

a moan as his fingers pressed along the sides of her throat, and my mouth drifted to her breasts.

"Yes, more," she whispered. Killian had one hand locked around her waist to keep her in place, and the other toyed with her air supply. She tilted her head down, and her eyes locked on me in a challenge stare - thank fuck they were still lavender, but now, I had work to do.

As Killian held her tight and fucked her from behind, I bent low. My tongue sucked at the base of his cock, my fingers cupping his balls and tapping at his asshole. He grunted, sliding her faster up and down his shaft. Then I buried my face in Carlyle's pussy, sucking her clit without mercy as Killian sped up even more.

I felt her orgasm rush through me, siphoning away my magic and stringing her body like a bow across Killian's muscled chest. He loosened his fingers, and a hoarse cry rattled from her throat just as the fae roared his release. I sat back on my knees, staring up at her.

Then I started scrambling because the snapping fangs and solid white eyes were back.

The dark-haired thing writhed in Killian's arms, and he yelled for Jai. Someone shoved the mirror close to the bed, and someone else twisted the creature's head toward it.

Because I couldn't call this thing *Carlyle*, even though I knew my girl had been right beneath my fingers only a second before.

"Jai, ice her," Killian shouted, his grip slipping despite Jack and Toro rushing in to help. I felt the jolt of Jai's ice magic in the air, and Carlyle slumped against Killian.

And it *was* Carlyle again - she'd changed so fast it made my head spin and my brain wonder if the world was playing tricks on me.

She groaned, shoving weakly at Killian and the others. "What the fuck, boss? Where did that even come from?"

She sounded like she would have been pissed if she weren't so weak, and suddenly, I felt like a fucking prick for my participation in whatever this had been.

Killian helped her settle back onto the bed, but he was looking as worried as I felt.

"Why is the mirror in here?" she asked, blinking at her reflection. "And were you all just, like, *watching*?"

"Did you see yourself in the mirror?" Jai asked, not answering any of her questions.

She shrugged. "I mean, yeah, I guess. But why? Answers, vampire."

Toro and Jack edged onto the bed. Jack was wide-eyed - he'd obviously finally seen the same thing as the rest of us. But why couldn't Carlyle? If she'd seen herself like that, we would be hearing about it.

"We have something to explain," Jai began, his voice actually shaded with embarrassment. He told the story quickly, and Carlyle's mouth was hanging open by the end of it.

"That's fucking nuts," she muttered, squinting at her reflection in the mirror. Then she glared at Jai. "Show me. In my mind."

I felt the crackle of ice again as he opened his memories to her. She shivered, and I reached over to wrap her in my arms. "I'm sorry, shortcake. I'm so sorry."

She grimaced. "Hey…you guys didn't do anything wrong. I mean it. I'm not mad. Weirded out a little, yeah." She shivered again, holding her stomach.

"Are you gonna hurl again?" Killian asked, sounding as chagrined as I felt. Even though she didn't think we'd done anything wrong, it still felt like we had.

But Carlyle shook her head, leaning into me. "I feel okay. I just wish I knew what the hell was going on with me. It's like I'm as sick as Haret was."

"We'll heal you, the same way you're healing Haret," Jack said, twining his fingers with hers.

"I don't know if I'm even doing that," she protested. "I'm screwing everything up, you guys."

"Hey, no," I rushed to reassure her. "Haret is just like anywhere else - it's made of individuals who sometimes do the wrong things. But it's also full of amazing people like you, who will always do the right things. We'll fix it all together, shortcake."

"Ugh," she moaned. "Even that *word* makes my stomach hurt. Who even am I if sugar makes me vomit?"

I chuckled. "It won't last. We'll figure out what's

going on with your body. I mean, we're pretty good at figuring out what it likes, right? Do you feel any stronger yet?"

She smiled and tilted her head. "Yeah, a little. But it's like I'm not absorbing much of your magic, even though I felt you give me so much."

"We'll figure it out, baby," Jack repeated, and the others crowded in to say the same. Just as we were tangling into a group hug, a popping in the room announced Dair's return.

"I brought your favorites," he called, raising a box filled with fresh pastries. The smell was wonderful, but-

"Oh, fuck," Carlyle cried, scrambling over limbs and vomiting over the side of the bed. "Goddamn it," she moaned, but soon she was giggling at herself, and even more at Dair's confused expression.

Wiping her mouth on the edge of Jack's offered sleeve, she grinned at us all. "I might be broken, but with my mates around me, I feel like I'm still beautiful - and strong." She held up the sunrise moonstone. "And I'll get back all your beautiful orange swirl of magic, Sol, I promise. *Nothing* is coming between my lion and me."

"Damn it, short-, I mean, damn it, Carlyle," I stuttered, trying to avoid her pet name. "I love you."

"I love you *all* so fucking much," she said, sighing and leaning back into the pillows. "Now, someone tell the mage about all the fun new fuckery we have in store. And then I want seconds of whatever strength potion you can give me." She winked at me, and my heart roared with pride that this amazing girl called herself mine.

WANT MORE?

This mystery continues soon in the next installment of *Sugar Bites* – a set of novellas chronicling the shenanigans Carlyle and her men get up to in their happily-ever-after.

Keep up-to-date and find Laurel and the Piece of Qilin fans in the Facebook reader group
LOVERS OF HARET.
https://www.facebook.com/groups/676410892715276/

Join Laurel's newsletter for new release information, sales, and special, sexy bonus content.
https://laurelchaseauthor.com/newsletter/

REVIEWS

Please consider leaving an honest review on your favorite reading and retail sites.
Lots of readers depend on reviews and recommendations to find their next read.

Love, Laurel

LaurelChaseAuthor.com

AUTHOR'S LOVE NOTE

Dear Reader,

Some of this is repeated from last time, but I really mean it, lol! I want to thank *you* first and forever.

If it weren't for your encouraging comments and hot character pics in our Lovers of Haret group and your amazing shares and reviews, I would never have thought to continue Carlyle's story past the initial series.

Thanks for making all of this so much fun! I haven't just found readers with this series, I've found friends.

Much love to Alisha and the Mod Squad (Belinda, Holly, Jacquie, Jesika, Laura, Leanne, and Nikki), who keep me entertained with tiktok clips and makeup tips. And eternal respect for my shy editor, my cover designer (Christian Bentulan), my betas (Cecily, Alisha, Leanne, and Laura), and my ARC team. I'm so grateful for all your hard – and fast – work and help.

And of course, kisses to my family and our very own pet unicorn, Mochi.

Stay sexy and sweet, Lovers!

See you next book!

Love, Laurel

ABOUT THE AUTHOR

Laurel Chase lives in the state that boasts of fast
horses, fast cars, and fast women.
She writes steamy romance and lives in her head more
and more each day – hey, the scenery is great in there.
She never sleeps enough, and she drinks too much
coffee, but she'd never replace any of that with
sensible stuff.

Find her hanging out on social media,
usually in the Lovers of Haret readers' group!